WILL

AMERICA

FAIL?

RYAN HOUCK

A POST HILL PRESS book

ISBN (Hardcover): 978-1-61868-9-474
ISBN (eBook): 978-1-61868-9-481

Cover by Travis Franklin

Post Hill
PRESS

Post Hill Press
109 International Drive, Suite 300
Franklin, TN 37067
Posthillpress.com

TABLE OF CONTENTS

To Jennifer

WILL

AMERICA

FAIL?

INTRODUCTION

"You're headlining Drudge."

"Seriously?"

Bigger than the front page of *The New York Times*, topping *The Drudge Report* was like having your headline carved in the moon—everyone saw it.

"Yeah, above the fold. Top billing." My friend was oddly matter-of-fact. "Drudge pulled the headline straight from your video—*'economic suicide pact.'*"

Print newspapers are on their way out. Dying, if not dead.

But you wouldn't know it to hear antiquated print lingo, like "above the fold," still bandied about by people who get most of their news online. I suppose terms of art occasionally outlast the art itself.

Three weeks prior, I'd huddled with two colleagues, John Sowinski and Tre' Evers, to sketch out a new video project we'd begun calling, *"If I Wanted America to Fail."* After the third draft, I was nervous. It broke most of the cardinal rules: Too dark—but dead-on accurate. Too long—but we couldn't find anything to cut. Too controversial—but it sure as hell had to be said.

The soon-to-be-viral video took aim at environmentalism run amok—*on Earth Day*. Off the air, one radio host told me, "That took balls." Just brains. It simply said what we'd all been thinking, fearing: *Our country is slipping away.*

Our inspiration was Paul Harvey's 1965 essay, *"If I Were the Devil."* In it, the famous radioman slipped into the shoes of Satan himself to imagine what plots the Prince of Darkness might contrive to corrupt mankind. After recounting a litany of contemporary social and civic ills, Harvey concludes: "If I were the Devil [...] I guess I would leave things pretty much the way they are."

Our conclusion was similar: *"If I Wanted America to fail,"* I said. "I suppose I wouldn't change a thing." This somber endnote would lead many observers to conclude my message was one of despair.

Not so.

The American Interest's Josef Joffe got it right when he noted that warnings of America's decline are intended to be "self-*defeating* prophecy." "We foretell" so that we may "forestall;" the goal is to break the spell, to change the course, to spur individuals to heroic action.[1]

And that is exactly what is needed now: *Heroic action.*

I'm a young man—27 years old when *"If I Wanted America to Fail"* went viral—and I'm very much counting on heroic action to turn things around; to do what Americans have done so often throughout our history: Beat expectations. Make a comeback.

Our video made its YouTube debut to a tiny audience on a damp Thursday night. We were approaching the Earth Day weekend and, when I left the office that evening, *"If I Wanted America to Fail"* had scarcely earned over 200 hits. Within less than two weeks, it would rack up over 2 million.

Seven days later, I'd find our video catapulted not just to the top of Matt Drudge's eponymous website but plastered across cable news outlets and replayed by leading talk radio hosts across the country. That very week, hungry and late for lunch, I stepped into my car, tuned the radio to AM540 and heard a familiar voice describe a new video suddenly sweeping the web.

"It's brilliant!" thundered Rush. "It absolutely nails the wacko environmentalist movement." A fixture of conservative households for two generations, Rush Limbaugh's voice was instantly recognizable.

"No way," I whispered to myself. "I think he's talking about us.'"

He was. Later that week, interviews with conservative titans Glenn Beck and John Stossel cemented the video's status as a new "conservative manifesto," as Fox News' Eric Bolling put it.

"If I Wanted America to Fail" went viral because it articulated an idea that many Americans had felt but couldn't quite express. I received plenty of hate mail when it and subsequent videos were released. I still do. However, the majority of mail is decidedly thoughtful and heartfelt. It comes from immensely decent and honest Americans across the country. Many have Millennial children, roughly my age.

They're worried about their kids; they're worried about the country those kids will soon inherit. The question they ask me is almost always the same:

"So, *honestly*, will America fail?"

I make no apologies: From the pen of a pessimist, this book is the unlikely *case for hope.* It is tempered optimism courtesy of a young smartass (me) better known for his gloom than his glee—and it may be hard to stomach for some of my fellow conservatives, for whom gloom and doom now feels quite natural. Of course, the gloom is understandable, even if the doom is premature. With a staggering $17 trillion national debt linked to a rising China, persistently high unemployment, and a stubbornly slow economic recovery, Americans have precious little left in the way of our trademark optimism.

That's led to some pretty tough questions, chief among them: Will America Fail?

Is America, like Rome before it, destined to crumble and collapse? Has the Information Age rendered the values of our Founders obsolete? Will our addiction to debt enslave us to China? Is the next generation of Americans—the so-called "Millennials"—prepared to lead?

The fear of American decline is now a recurring hot topic on primetime cable news programs and daytime talk radio shows. Public opinion polls routinely report that once-devoutly-hopeful Americans have grown deeply pessimistic about our country's future. Gradually, the fear of American decline has begun to reshape the political landscape.

This fear is deepest among conservatives.

For many, the 2012 Election seemed like the last chance to stop a leftwing agenda aimed at rewriting our cultural DNA. Terms such as "Makers and Takers" and "the 47 percent" became watchwords of this struggle. We cast the election as a make or break moment—a point of no return. If Barack Obama saw his 2008 election as "the moment when the rise of the oceans began to slow and our planet began to heal," then conservatives saw the 2012 race in terms no less consequential. This, we thought, was the moment when our movement would either be vindicated or vanquished, when the American Experiment would either survive or fail. For many conservatives, Barack Obama's reelection seemed to seal our fate.

I was one of those conservatives.

I belong to the generation that returned Barack Obama to the White House. I also belong to the generation that has suffered most deeply during his presidency. In the weeks following the 2012 Elections, I struggled to escape the feeling that our country had been lost—that this was no ordinary election; that it was a the symptom of a deeper disease; that we had become sick, addicted to the narcotic of entitlement. The GOP's suddenly sober efforts to ship us off to rehab were woefully inadequate compared to progressives' seductive pill pushing. Leftwing pundits crowed that this was the end of the GOP. A new "Coalition of the Ascendant," comprised of Millennials, minorities and single women, would sweep out the stodgy Republican remnants and inaugurate a new age of liberalism, they said.

It was tempting to believe them.

There can be no doubt that our movement and our country face grave challenges. As a writer and producer, I've certainly spent plenty of time—in front of the camera and behind it—ringing the alarm bell, like many others. In the space of only a few days, millions of Americans watched "*If I Wanted America to Fail*" and were moved by its bleak, seemingly pessimistic prophecy of America's decline.

For that reason, I've been called a "Declinist"—one who predicts and revels in forecasts of America's doom. I'm not. On the contrary, I am well aware that people are not passive observers of history— we are free agents, with the power to shape the contours of history. But like many who read this book, I spent the latter part of 2012 fearful that the once-bright light of American Exceptionalism was failing.

By the time the New Year rolled around, I decided to take a closer look at the forces shaping my generation. Why did we vote for Barack Obama and are we now reliable foot soldiers for his seductive brand of statism? My search quickly widened to include broader economic and cultural trends. Will America emerge from its self-imposed stagnation? Will China "own us" because it owns our debt? Will this rising dragon unseat the United States as the world's leading power?

I believe that things are shifting in the shadows; that powerful underlying trends— cultural, political, and economic—are converging to halt decline and renew hope. A time of terrible difficulty is ahead, but just beyond it, there is a *Turning Point*.

My call: America will not fail. Conservatism will not die. Millennials will not forever form the backbone of Barack Obama's *Coalition of the Ascendant*. Buoyed by long-term economic forces and powered by a Promethean spark, Millennials will help forge a 21st Century that belongs to the United States. They will not belong to any political party. And they will not preside over the collapse of conservatism; they will reshape it in their image.

For many conservatives who watched with dismay as my generation twice elected Barack Obama, this scenario will seem hard to believe; my optimism, Pollyannaish at best. To those conservatives, I would say, *read on.* This book isn't based on a single snapshot in time; it's not based on the disappointment of a single election; it's not based on Millennials' politics—it's based on Millennials' culture, which will ultimately shape their politics.

Change is afoot—and not just the kind you can slap on a bumper sticker.

To evaluate that change, I'll address the *Five Pillars of American Power*, which form the bedrock of US prosperity and the basis for an American-led international order. The first pillar: *Economic Dynamism*—America's innovation-based economy, which relies upon on free enterprise, entrepreneurship, and creative destruction; second, *Cultural Universality*—the powerful, naturally *American* qualities that also have broad global appeal, such as the values of personal choice and free speech; third, *Domestic Stability*—shaped by key civic and demographic factors, including healthy demographics, democratic institutions, and the Rule of Law; fourth, *Energy Security*—our country's ability to fuel its economy, particularly with domestic energy reserves; and fifth, *Military Primacy*—America's ability to deter adversaries, support allies, and wage war.

Although some of these pillars may now appear cracked, *three important events* will take place over the next two decades, which will seal the cracks, mend the trusses, and strengthen America's 21st Century foundations: First, America's Millennials—an entrepreneurial generation—will pioneer a new politics, inherit the nation's great institutions, and then remake them; Second, *the Great Transition* from the Industrial Age to the Information Age—which long ago transformed private life—will finally reach the halls of government, bringing about renewed stability and growth; Third, the transformative power of technology, which has already changed the world, will fragment America's *Three Cultural Drivers*—entertainment, education, and the news media—that shape our national politics. By 2035, the United States will have overcome its growing pains, achieved energy independence, adapted to a new model of government, enjoyed something of a conservative renaissance, and reached new heights of prosperity.

A note: While this book is optimistic, it has no guarantees, only probabilities and prescriptions. It's grounded in our history and our position relative to economic and geopolitical rivals. It's based on a view from 30,000 feet up, over a long period of time. It's not about a single presidency or a single policy. It's not intended as a license to stick our heads in the sand or become content with the status quo. It is a push; a prod; a provocation—and all the while a reminder that, to borrow from Mr. Joffe, our country's recent backward steps may, unexpectedly, give us just enough room for a running start.[2]

CHAPTER 1
HANG ONTO THAT TOWEL

Every society has both *hardware* and *software*.

Culture is a society's hardware. It encompasses such things as a nation's history, values, and worldview. This social hardware also incorporates bedrock economic, environmental, and geographic realities. For example, whether or not a nation has abundant natural resources or tends to believe in a higher power is indicative of its culture—its hardware. These matters speak to a society's broader architecture and are typically transformed only by catastrophic, tumultuous events.

Politics is a society's software. It's the operating system we're running *at the moment*—Democrat, Republican and so forth. Undoubtedly, poor software can underutilize excellent hardware. Poor software can also ensure that certain applications—free enterprise, common decency, education and the like—don't work properly.

Right now, our software sucks. But our hardware still kicks ass.

America is currently running a deeply problematic, buggy, and inadequate software, designed and distributed by the Left. Countless patches and updates haven't made this sluggish operating system any better. A bloated and activist federal government, dysfunctional public education system, troubling deficits, and fabulously lackluster leadership have combined to make this American machine run very, very slowly.

Fortunately, the *Five Pillars of American Power—Economic Dynamism, Domestic Stability, Military Primacy, Energy Security* and *Cultural Universality*—are based largely on our cultural architecture, on our *hardware*. That's important because hardware—culture—can outlast presidents and overcomes politics.

To understand the nature and durability of our American hardware, I'll ask the gentlemen to roll up those suit sleeves and invite the ladies to slip in those shoulder pads—we're headed back to 1989.

Irony is alive and well as the Soviet Union—a communist empire that supposedly represents the workers of the world—suffers a wave of crippling work stoppages. In Soviet-dominated Czechoslovakia, a brewery worker named Zdenek Janicek steps onto a platform and begins to speak. [3]

"We hold these truths to be self-evident," he says, "that all men are created equal, that they are endowed by their creator with certain unalienable rights, that among these are life, liberty, and the pursuit of happiness. Americans understood these rights more than 200 years ago. We are only now learning to believe that we are entitled to the same rights." [4]

Bigger than baseball and bolder than jazz, the Declaration of Independence may be the best, most concentrated expression of American values ever conceived. Yet, it was not an original idea. The Declaration sought neither "originality of principle or sentiment" yet was not "copied from any particular and previous writing." It was, as Jefferson put it, "intended to be an expression of the American mind." [5]

This is the privilege of a people forged by philosophy rather than geography; to gather up the best ideas mankind has to offer and to devise a *new hardware*. Not a crudely improvised analogue contraption based on a common race or religion; but a wonderfully *intentional* new digital hardware based on a common theory of liberty.

Liberty is the very fire that animates the human race. America did not invent it. *It* invented America. This *idea* makes our country bigger than its borders; it has made our *intentional* nation an *accidental* superpower—at its best, virtuous, just, and free. *Liberty*—the modern vernacular is *personal choice*—is what America offers the world. It is our value proposition, our unique selling point, our sales pitch—our guiding philosophy.

And it is the basis for our record-breaking, standard-setting *hardware*.

It is why we exist. It is why Zdenek Janicek quoted Jefferson. It is why our values retain universal appeal. It is why the *Five Pillars of American Power* endured great calamities and failed presidents in the past—and why they will endure this failed president, too.

Welcome back to 2014—where our *software* sucks.

The reelection of Barack Obama has convinced many

conservatives that we're on the Highway to Hell with no off-ramps in sight. While conservatives' causes for concern are many, five key concerns threaten the *Five Pillars of American Power*: First, the growth of the welfare state and its consequences for private virtue, productivity and, ultimately, *Domestic Stability*; Second, the rise of China and the threat it poses to US *Military Primacy*; Third, the swell of the regulatory state and its crippling impact on free enterprise, namely those companies responsible for our *Energy Security*; Fourth, the erosion of US prestige and its impact on American *Cultural Universality*; and fifth, the crushing national debt—much of it owned by foreign powers, such as China—and the toll it takes on America's *Economic Dynamism.*

There is no greater threat than the national debt, the tendrils of which snake into the foundations of every *pillar of power.* Excessive national debt drains dollars from private investment, saps *Economic Dynamism,* impedes US foreign policy objectives, and threatens—as evidenced by Chinese saber-rattling in Southeast Asia—America's long-term *Domestic Stability* and, ultimately, *Military Primacy.*

Debt is the destroyer of nations.

That may sound pretty Old Testament—but it's true. And it's what keeps conservatives up at night. Not only does our national debt imperil the prosperity of our children, it limits US military options abroad and binds us to foreign creditors with conflicting geopolitical interests. That's why many consider the issues of "debt" and "China" inextricably linked.

If America fails, debt will almost certainly be the overriding reason.

At more than $17 trillion, US national debt already amounts to over $50,000 for every man, woman and child in the country—more than $1.1 million for every *taxpayer.*[6] Spending on Social Security, Medicaid, and Medicare alone total nearly 45 percent of the federal budget—and these programs are growing, not shrinking. Combined, Medicare and Social Security have racked up more than $47.5 trillion in unfunded liabilities—that's the amount of money these programs will someday owe but be unable to pay. President Obama commissioned a bipartisan panel to study and recommend solutions to this crisis. When the panel's recommendations were issued, he promptly ignored them. Then, he proposed a budget that *never* balances.[7]

Debt is not new. However, the current level of peacetime debt is unprecedented.

Typically, debt increases (sometimes dramatically) during periods of crisis, namely war. The United States incurred roughly

$75 million of debt (about 30 percent of GDP) after the Revolutionary War. Debt fell until the War of 1812 broke out in, well, 1812—at which point it rose again sharply. Only once, in 1835, has the US been debt-free. That lasted until 1836, at which point debt began to accrue once more. Just prior to the Civil War, debt totaled nearly $65 million. But two years into the war, federal debt vaulted past $1 billion. By the end of the war, it was approaching $3 billion (also about 30 percent of GDP). Late-century economic growth fueled by industrialization helped America pay down its Civil War debts. However, debt would spike again during World War I (to roughly—you guessed it—30 percent of GDP). When the roaring twenties followed, debt quickly fell. Although public spending increased during the Great Depression, it was not until World War II that debt began to reach truly stratospheric levels. By the end of the war, US national debt totaled $260 billion—or roughly 113 percent of Gross Domestic Product (GDP), the highest it has ever been.[8]

Today, total US national debt is roughly 70 percent of GDP—and much higher if you count debt owed to federal programs, like Social Security. While not record-setting, that figure is certainly excessive for peacetime. High peacetime debt undermines US *Military Primacy* by limiting our military and diplomatic options abroad. For example, it's difficult to deter foreign aggressors who know that we are financially constrained. A large national debt also dampens *Economic Dynamism* by sucking financial capital out of private investment markets, which would otherwise be used to fund economic expansion. Unless our entitlement programs—Social Security, Medicare, and Medicaid—are reformed, the national debt will reach truly unsustainable (and possibly irreversible) levels sometime in the 2030s.[9]

Strange as it sounds, Social Security is actually America's single largest creditor, owning about 16.5 percent of the debt load. The US Federal Reserve—America's Central Bank—is not far behind, with about 12.4 percent. China owns about 7.6 percent of the debt.[10]

And that's what is causing the sleepless nights.

Within the next two decades, one of two things will occur: We will either reform entitlement spending and place it on a sustainable course or it will choke the federal budget, bringing about truly draconian cuts to vulnerable seniors, with the potential to cause serious social unrest, upending our country's *Domestic Stability*.

But don't toss in the towel yet.

America's debt problem is serious. However, debt conditions can change quickly—in good ways and bad. At the beginning of the 21st Century, America's debt reached a modern-low of roughly 30 percent. Observers often spoke of eliminating the national debt altogether within a single generation. The military spending that followed 9/11 combined with the expansion of Medicare and the collapse of the housing market quickly crushed that optimism. By the same token, America has managed to subdue debt during periods of economic expansion—in the late 18th Century, the late 19th Century, the 1920s, and the 1990s. Our country has proven strong enough to survive confidence-shaking recessions, misery-inducing depressions, globe-spanning wars, and even terrible presidents in the past. There are two reasons the *Five Pillars of American Power* have survived (albeit weaker) the reckless spending and lackluster recovery of Barack Obama's presidency:

First, the United States is stable (relatively speaking) and Uncle Sam has never been a deadbeat. Through thick and thin, we've always paid up. We're also free of sectarian violence, coup d'états, and general social instability—no military juntas or kangaroo courts over the past two-and-a-half centuries. Until recently, America's national debt has also been comparatively low. At present, it's bad—but others are far worse. Japan, for example, has a national debt well over 200 percent of GDP, more than double that of the United States. Even Germany, which is often considered fiscally responsible, has a debt-to-GDP ratio of slightly more than 80 percent. Meanwhile, as I'll cover in greater depth in the *Turning Point*, China, far from owning the United States, is afflicted by deep-seeded troubles of its own. The Peoples' Republic's distressed banking sector may be on the brink of a dangerous new bubble that could dwarf America's 2008 housing calamity. In the aftermath of the Great Recession, China's overall debt-to-GDP soared from 150 percent to more than 200 percent today, thanks mostly to local governments and state-backed companies.[11]

There's a second reason towel-tossing would be premature: Size. Economically, the US is big—*really big.* That's made the dollar more durable. Faced with instability, investors flock to the dollar because it offers unparalleled liquidity, which, in a crisis, is king. America is so big, in fact, that foreign countries, banks, hedge funds, and billionaires with excess cash can safely park it in US Treasuries without disrupting the market or risking their principal.

This advantage has made the US dollar the world's reserve currency—another term for the paper that governments and institutions buy and frequently use for international transactions. For example, China buys dollars because it does an enormous amount of international trade, and international trade is denominated in US dollars.

That's why—despite irresponsible federal spending and unfunded entitlement liabilities—investors keep buying dollars. The high demand for dollars has suppressed the cost of borrowing. As a result, only 6 percent of the US budget is devoted to interest payments on the national debt. That's down from 15 percent in the mid-90s. [12] It's also why, in 2013, about 62 percent of the world's currency reserves were made up of dollars. In 1995, it was only about 59 percent. [13]

Although it makes our exports more expensive, the dollar's unique (though increasingly fragile) status as world reserve currency conveys what the French call *"exorbitant privilege."* Damn, it even sounds French when you write it in English.

Whatever you call it, the dollar's special importance affords Uncle Sam an uncommonly large margin for error, making it harder for our terrible political software to ruin our stellar cultural hardware. Basically, we get to make mistakes, even big ones (Barack Obama-sized mistakes, for example). That doesn't mean we're invincible. Just tougher than most.

One of the most troubling parts of the debt crisis—and it is a crisis—is the increasingly common misconception that it cannot be solved. Although they were shaken by the Great Recession and the amateurish, incompetent presidency of Barack Obama, the *Five Pillars of American Power* remain:

In terms of *Economic Dynamism,* the US easily outclasses its rivals. At the beginning of 2014, the American economy weighed in at around $17 trillion—still larger than the nominal GDP of all so-called BRIC nations—China, Russia, India, and Brazil—*combined.*[14] America is rich and, comparatively speaking, so are Americans. Despite being a very large economy, the US still boasts one of the world's highest per capita GDPs.

But traditional metrics like Gross Domestic Product (GDP) fail to fully capture the magnitude of American economic influence. Despite decades of rising competition, US firms lead 70 percent of the world's major economic sectors. America's lead is most pronounced in the industries of the future, such as computer hardware and software, health care, pharmaceuticals, and biotechnology. On average, American shareholders own roughly 85 percent of these leading US companies, explaining why over 40 percent of the world's total household wealth can be found in the United States.[15] Moreover, America is home to a workforce that is, comparatively speaking, highly educated, highly diverse, and highly productive. The United States ranks as the most innovative economy on the planet, turning in top-ten performances in R&D intensity, productivity, high-tech density, and researcher concentration.[16] Its H-Index score, which measures scientific impact, easily outstrips its closest competitors—most of whom are allies.[17]

Backed by its highly developed venture capital corps, the US is the birthplace of fully half of *Encyclopedia Britannica's* 321 *Great Inventions*, despite being a young country. In a single year, its exports exceed the entire Gross Domestic Product of Russia. Although it is no longer celebrated as a manufacturing economy, the United States is the world's second largest manufacturer—and it is now gaining, not losing ground. With less than 5 percent of the world's population, it is home to 60 percent of the world's top fifty universities, 40 percent of the world's billionaires, 30 percent of the world's millionaires, a third of the world's Nobel laureates, and a fourth of the world's Fortune 500 companies, more than twice that of any other nation.[18] [19] [20] Its economy represents roughly one-fifth of the world's GDP.[21] While foreign investments in the US total roughly $2.5 trillion, American investments abroad total roughly $3.3 trillion—and both are roughly twice that of any other country.[22] Compared to others, Americans are big believers in hard work: 77 percent say that most people can succeed if they work hard, compared with 59 percent of those surveyed in emerging countries, 55 percent of those in Arab countries and 50 percent in European countries.[23] Despite the best efforts of its worst political leaders, America is still ranked near the top of the various economic indices that measure competitiveness and ease of doing business.

When it comes to *Energy Security*, a revolution is underway beneath our feet.

Despite an out-of-control Environmental Protection Agency (EPA) that seems bent on crushing domestic energy development, the free market has proven resilient. The United States has seen its oil production increase by more than 50 percent over the last 8 years, faster than any other country on Earth. Over the same period, domestic natural gas production has soared by more than 30 percent. [24] The US already holds the largest recoverable coal reserves in the world and became the leading producer of natural gas while I was writing this book. By the time it is published, America will have also unseated Saudi Arabia as the planet's top producer of oil.[25]

In terms of *Military Primacy*, America has spent much of the last century designing the world order it desires. Now, it must simply defend that order. And, militarily, it remains positioned to do so. In terms of defense spending, military technology and power projection capabilities, the United States surpasses all potential rivals.

Although its competitors are catching up, US defense spending still dwarfs that of its nearest rival, China, roughly 5-to-1. Indeed, America spends more than the next 10 countries combined, most of which are treaty allies.[26] Despite recent cuts, the United States has as many aircraft carriers as the rest of the world *combined*. Single US carrier groups outclass the entire navies and air forces of most other countries. The US Air Force is easily the largest and most technologically advanced on the planet—as is the US Navy. America maintains a military presence in roughly 150 of the world's 192 countries at any given time, including large deployments in Germany, Japan, South Korea, Italy, and the United Kingdom, totaling nearly 80,000 active duty personnel in Europe and nearly 50,000 in East Asia and the Pacific. While recent defense cuts threaten America's ability to deter potential rivals, no other country presently comes close to matching US power projection capabilities or sophisticated alliance systems.

Moreover, the US enjoys a favorable geography with unrestricted access to both of the world's major oceans, the Atlantic and the Pacific. North America is one of the largest and most peaceful free trade zones in the world. Despite recurring immigration and drug-related tensions with Mexico, the United States enjoys comparatively cordial relations with both of its immediate neighbors, neither of whom harbor global aspirations of their own. Contrast this with the geopolitical challenges faced by America's emerging rival, China. Hemmed in by mountains and constrained by its suspicious neighbors, China's ambitions have aroused regional mistrust rather than cooperation. This mistrust has strengthened America's Pacific alliance system and will impede China's ability to influence global affairs.

When it comes to *Domestic Stability,* the United States faces troubling levels of public distrust of traditional institutions. However, the US is unlikely to go the way of Rome—at least not within my lifetime. Every so often, Americans are treated to a budget showdown or debt ceiling spectacle, in which our elected leaders careen the ship of state toward the very precipice of disaster, just before returning it safely to calm waters. Understandably, such incidents engender feelings of dismay and even despair among many Americans. Yet, these reasonably tame, reasonably civil disagreements are notable for their lack of bloodshed.

Yes, *bloodshed.*

As much as we rightly decry political dysfunction and executive overreach, our constitutional system of checks and balances, though battered and bruised, endures. Imagine if an angry senator sought to raise an army, rather than a campaign war chest, or if a president dissolved the Congress and closed the courts. Compare our rather subdued conflicts to Rome's "Crisis of the Third Century," when roughly two-dozen claimants vied for the imperial throne and the empire was torn into three parts. In the years preceding the crisis, Rome suffered humiliating military defeats, plague, and political assassination. Despite being crippled by Germanic invasions and long-lasting economic turmoil, Rome would emerge from this crisis and regain its place as the preeminent power in the region for another century. It's fashionable to assert that we're doomed. However, by the Roman measure, American crises—with their notable absence of warfare and dictatorships—are quite tame. And America's setbacks, by the same measure, are quite small.

Barack Obama's pledge to use his "pen" and his "phone" to govern by executive order rang all kinds of alarm bells. Justifiably so. The nature, if not the number, of the president's executive orders suggests that our law professor-in-chief has precious little love of the constitution he is sworn to uphold (and professes to understand). However, controversial executive orders are about as durable as a disposable diaper. This president's executive orders, like those of his predecessors, are written in the sand—easily washed away by his successor or the courts.

Lastly, it is in the area of *Cultural Universality* that America's influence is perhaps most pronounced. Thanks to its top-notch cultural hardware, American marketing, movies, music, and art have displaced Rome's legions. The rise of the Internet has extended this influence, serving as yet another vehicle for the delivery of American culture and values. A testament to this truth: The number of democracies around the globe has risen by over 50 percent in the last 25 years.[27]

A Greek friend told me, "You Americans don't even realize it: Your greatest export is your culture. Everyone wants jeans and Coca-Cola." Can America's cultural influence be reduced to soda and denim—some sort of trendy, affordable materialism?

Call it pop philosophy on the cheap, but there's something to it.

US corporations export American brands and, by extension, culture. Advertisements, online video content, and major motion pictures are also vehicles that promote our way of life around the world. Foreign viewers who may never visit Los Angeles, New York, or Miami can see it on TV. But, you might say, aren't our best cultural ambassadors still our oldest? Franklin, Jefferson, Lincoln? Certainly, these figures left a powerful legacy that continues to influence governments across the globe. There's also little doubt that the words of great Americans have inspired democratic revolutions in places suffering under the darkest tyrannies. Lincoln's Gettysburg Address, King's "I Have a Dream" speech, FDR's "Nothing to Fear But Fear Itself" speech, and Reagan's "Tear Down This Wall" speech have left their mark as well.

But this isn't what my Greek friend meant. She wasn't referring to America's Founders or political titans, but rather to a very basic form of the philosophy that inspired them: The idea of choice; the right to purchase freely; the right to express openly; the power to govern one's self. In a nutshell: Liberty.

As I said before, America did not invent this idea; it was invented by it. "Jeans and Coca-Cola" are merely modern proxies for these ancient but timeless notions of liberty. This simple explanation for American culture may offend some. Not me. American government was devised by man's intellect, but American culture was born of something very central to the human soul: The desire to determine one's own destiny. This desire knows no particular religion; it knows no particular creed; it knows no particular race or ethnicity. It is *universal*. Liberty is not an American idea—it is a human impulse, harnessed *by* Americans; and it speaks directly to the aspiration of every human heart.

That is *Cultural Universality*. And it endures.

Jeans and Coca-Cola represent more than clothing and soft drinks. They are products of an elastic but durable form of freedom, which observers have catalogued for centuries. America's unique blend of cultural, economic, and military might has forged an international system based on free trade, which no serious rival seeks to replace. In this way, America has created a more durable empire than the Romans ever did.

As a result, the *Five Pillars of American Power* have weathered the Great Recession. They will even survive Barack Obama. It's no time to toss in the towel, no time to give up. Despite recent stresses to the tresses, American might is still far more complete than that of any superpower to precede it. Josef Joffe sums it up:

At the pinnacle of British power (1870), the country's GDP was separated from that of its rivals by mere percentages. The United States dwarfs the rest, even China, by multiples—be it in terms of GDP, nuclear weapons, defense spending, projection forces, R&D outlays, or patent applications. Seventeen of the world's top universities are American; this is where tomorrow's intellectual capital is being produced. America's share of global GDP has held steady for forty years, while Europe's, Japan's and Russia's have shrunk. And China's miraculous growth is slipping, echoing the fates of the earlier Asian dragons (Japan, South Korea, Taiwan) that provided the economic model: high savings, low consumption, "exports first." China is facing a disastrous demography; the United States, rejuvenated by steady immigration, will be the youngest country of the industrial world (after India). [28]

The United States faces headwinds: A bad president, truly troubling levels of public debt, declining trust in civic institutions. However, we're also buoyed by a bevy of underappreciated tailwinds. Three such tailwinds merit extra attention in this chapter, since they will factor heavily into this book's *Turning Point.*

First, Barack Obama sought to unravel Reagan's political legacy and revive America's FDR-era faith in big government. He failed.

The Obama presidency has offered a crash-course in the drawbacks of liberalism. Little more than a year after re-electing him, a mere 41 percent of young Americans—Millennials—approved of the president's job performance. 54 percent disapproved. In another bad sign for big government, 57 percent said they disapproved of Obamacare.[29] Over the long term, big government politics are incongruent with the values of thrift, individualism, and distrust of big institutions, which form the Millennial DNA. Expect support for big government to continue its decline over the next several years, as the Obamacare debacle slowly unfolds. Of course, the speed with which big government unravels depends on how often (and how successfully) the administration delays key provisions of its own foolish law. Yet, in unilaterally delaying wide-scale implementation of Obamacare, the president is establishing precedents that his successor—should it be a Republican—may use to dismantle the law entirely.

Second, and somewhat counter-intuitively, Millennials may be the first generation in recent American history to enjoy a rebirth of domestic manufacturing. Productivity—a measure of economic efficiency—steadily rose in the United States since the end of World War II. For a while, the average wage of the American worker rose along with it. But in the 1970s, the two lines began to diverge. Productivity continued to rise, while earnings stagnated. There are many reasons for flat wages, but increased competition from foreign manufacturers is one of the biggest. Recently, however, thanks to high US productivity combined with more competitive wages, greater access to abundant domestic energy, and shorter distances to market, manufacturing is beginning to return to the United States. The energy revolution is laying the groundwork for an American comeback with the potential to thrust our people to new heights of prosperity in the 2030s.

Third, China will suffer setbacks, opening the door to a resurgent mid-century America. China is not the first Asian dragon to challenge US *Military Primacy* in the Pacific or the first rising power to pose an economic threat to American dominance. Its sheer size may make it a match for the United States. However, as I'll explain in the *Turning Point*, China faces serious internal problems—including a potentially catastrophic demographic collapse that will only begin to unfold two decades from now. The United States, as I'll discuss, is well positioned to avoid a similar fate.

Right now, in the midst of Barack Obama's second-term malaise, this *Turning Point* certainly seems very far off. Indeed, it's all too easy to understand why today's politics—society's *software*—create hopelessness, particularly among conservatives. From the seemingly endless onslaught of new regulations, to the catastrophic conception and rollout of Obamacare, to the White House's constant insistence on saddling Americans with higher taxes, to the deadlocked Congress, unable to address the debt—people are tired, frustrated, and ready to give up hope.

It's time to dump this software; wipe this hard drive.

After all, the United States boasts world-class, history-making, standard-setting cultural hardware. Two centuries of liberty, vast natural resources, a deeply embedded spirit of entrepreneurship, enviable geography, and a robust civic tradition that favors personal initiative all coalesce to form a hardware that is incredibly durable and unlikely to be outclassed anytime in the 21st Century.

So before you toss in the towel on America, forget about the Left's buggy software for a moment; take yourself out of the status quo. Try to look at things from 30,000 feet up. Consider more than the temporary politics of the moment; remember that we've had terrible presidents before—and many were far more capable practitioners of their politics than Barack Obama. Our hardware is strong and liberty is not so fragile that one president can snuff it out. Yes, many fellow Americans were fooled. But history does not judge us by our immunity to mistakes. It judges us by our capacity for fixing them.

CHAPTER 2
MILLENNIALS: GENERATION CONTRADICTION

As befits the whole over-validated lot of us, we got to pick our own name.

Seriously, we did.

Neil Howe and William Strauss coined the term "Millennial" in their 2000 book, *Millennials Rising*, after learning it was the name preferred by young Americans themselves. Millennials were turned off by other names, such as "Echo Boomers" and "Generation Y" because such terms cast us in the shadow of prior generations.

Don't roll your eyes, Boomers. At least we didn't pick "Generation Awesome."

Of course, it's amusing that a generation buried in participation trophies and often derided as coddled, entitled, and narcissistic would be given the chance to choose its own name. Somehow, it's also fitting. After all, nothing is nearer to the heart of this build-your-own-playlist generation than the idea of *choice*. More on that later.

There are a lot of strong, popular opinions about Millennials. Some say they're a throng of lazy, tech-addled moochers. Others say they're a smart, civic-minded chorus of cloud-hopping visionaries. Fine, but let's save the myth busting (or myth-confirming) for later. This chapter is a fact-finding mission.

Regardless of how Millennials got the name, we're now the largest living generation, comprising somewhere between 78 and 82 million Americans, depending upon who you choose to count. By 2017, Millennials—typically considered those born between 1980 and 2000, will have more spending power than any other generation.[30]   By 2020, we will make up nearly 40 percent of the electorate.[31]

Most Millennials were born during an era of unprecedented peace and prosperity. Our parents elected Ronald Reagan and Bill Clinton, though most of us were too young to vote for (or be heavily influenced by) either president. In 2000, early-wave Millennials roughly split their vote between Al Gore and George W. Bush. These voters then came of age during the dark days of September 11th, 2001. At first, these events inspired a surge of patriotism among young Americans and an acceptance of tougher security measures aimed at preventing further terrorist attacks.

It didn't last. Two protracted foreign wars and one Great Recession later Millennials had largely soured on the muscular foreign policy of the Bush years and rejected most of the administration's domestic policy agenda as well. To Boomers, Ronald Reagan—the *Great Communicator*—carried the torch for conservatism. However, Reagan was to Millennials what John F. Kennedy was to Boomers: An iconic president they are just too young to really remember. To Millennials, the only visible GOP standard-bearer—the president who, for all practical purposes, embodied the conservative movement—was George W. Bush.

Yikes.

In 2008, Barack Obama's election became the empty vessel for Millennials' wholesale repudiation of the Bush years. This moment represented the high tide of their great expectations. Then-Senator Obama's simple, vacuous slogan of "Yes, we can!" seemed to stupefy hordes of eager young rally-goers, desperate for a taste of something different.

But Millennials are not a loyal bunch. Shortly after returning Barack Obama to the White House in 2012, they began to abandon the president they put in power—with long-term political consequences for the country.

Of course, the Millennial's current *political* worldview was shaped by 9/11, two prolonged foreign conflicts, and the back-to-back, two-term presidencies of George W. Bush and Barack Obama. However, the better indicator of Millennials' future politics is not their present politics—it's their culture. And on a *cultural* level, three key factors distinguish Millennials from other generations: First, the tech-effect—Millennials' reliance on personal technology and the various cultural quirks produced by such reliance; second, the Great Recession, which serves as the Millennial's formative economic experience; and third, expectations—which started out uncommonly high among this generation of young Americans.

Let's start with the tech-effect. It is no surprise that Millennials are tech-savvy—some might say, tech-obsessed. However, their fixation on personal gadgetry is unique only when compared to prior generations, who are more likely to view such technology as novel. It is altogether likely that the members of every generation to follow mine will wrap their daily lives in personal technology, too. This generational feature may seem strange (and irksome) to our parents and grandparents, but it will appear quite normal to our children and grandchildren, as is often the case with significant advances in technology.

I bet the horse-drawn carriage crowd didn't care for the first car drivers either.

That's certainly not an excuse for the side-effects of overstimulation—such as texting at dinner or cruising Facebook at work—which can be intensely irritating generational shortcomings. And speaking of which, if you're an ethically challenged Millennial and you've pirated this book online to peruse in your cubicle, two things: First, thanks for the interest. But second, grow a conscience, send me a check (PayPal works, too), and get back to work—Obama's counting on his cut.

While they're in their cubicles, no doubt pirating scintillating literature, Millennials are also more likely than prior generations to create a social networking profile, post a video online, or own a cell phone without a landline. Younger Millennials are also more likely to text, tweet and post videos than older Millennials. They're more likely to visit social networking sites repeatedly throughout the day. About 30 percent of Millennials with a social networking profile make multiple visits a day, with slightly more than half saying they visit at least once a day. Similarly, Millennials are the only age group in which a majority reports connecting to the Internet wirelessly while away from home or work. [32]

While most Americans think new technology makes life easier, it's not surprising that its youngest adopters are most comfortable with it. Twice as many members of the Silent Generation bemoan new technology as Millennials—36 percent to 18 percent. [33] The Millennial cannot remember a time when news was not available 24 hours a day, seven days a week. In basements and garages across the country, our parents tinkered with the very first personal computers, eventually giving birth to the Information Age—and later, us.

As a result, many Millennials were raised with computers in their homes. By the time we reached adulthood, personal technology had become fully integrated into our lives—almost as important as a microwave and easily more important than an oven. (Seriously, who uses those?) Today, we expect technology to work. Right *now*. No excuses. And we feel little loyalty to companies or institutions that cannot keep up.

Love it or hate it, the society we grew up in is quite different from that of our parents. It's much flatter, typified by less hierarchy, less structure, and greater access to information. In this new world, the Internet has been a liberating, empowering new frontier—a Wild West, in many ways—a great democratizing force.

Today, young Americans with a professional interest can easily pursue it through sprawling, Internet-based social networks that make it easier to chase passions or business aspirations (or both). Many of the barriers are gone. We're free to take alternative paths to the marketplace, the social space, or the entertainment world. Aspiring authors have eBooks, aspiring filmmakers have YouTube, aspiring journalists have online blogging, and so on. While many generations avail themselves of technology, Millennials are the first adult generation to come of age in this new ecosystem.

Millennials' reliance on social media and online communication of every form—coupled with the Recession-era discrediting of major government and business institutions—has created a unique set of circumstances. Young Americans no longer trust "big" *anything*. Big banks, big religion, and lately, even big government, have fallen out of favor as Millennials have watched time-honored institutions falter and fail during the Great Recession.

And that's the second major factor that distinguishes Millennials.

Since becoming adults, they've seen the economy crumble, jobs vanish and the life savings of older Americans evaporate. Young Americans found their expectations for happiness and prosperity shattered just as they bounded into the job market, high on youthful "takeover-the-world" vim and vigor. Now, they're scared. Nearly 90 percent say that the economy affects their daily life with close to half cutting spending on food and skipping vacation. A third are seeking second-jobs while a quarter have downgraded their living situation. Most importantly, 84 percent say they had to delay major life changes because of the economy. According to researchers, the economic experiences of Millennials tend to align more closely with their Depression-era grandparents and great grandparents, than their Boomer parents.[34]

As is commonly reported, more young Americans now live with their parents than when Boomers were coming of age. *The Washington Post* reports that 32 percent of young people lived with their parents in 1968 compared with 36 percent today. This 4 percent uptick is largely explained by three factors: First, the less-than-stellar job market, which has persisted throughout the Obama years; second, a higher percentage of college-bound kids, who are counted as living at home; and third, a corollary of the second, more student loan debt, which has caused a higher number of "failures to launch."[35]

The near-necessity of a post-secondary education has not only loaded up young Americans with dangerous levels of debt, it has also delayed major life decisions that tend to correlate with financial independence (and political evolution)—namely job-acquisition and family formation.   Forty years ago, when fewer young adults attended college, the percentage of dorm-dwellers was considerably smaller.   Upon graduating high school, more young people immediately entered the workforce.   As a result, job-acquisition, financial independence, and marriage came at a younger age.

At the same time, the labor market was far more favorable to young Americans carrying no more than a high school degree. Today, on the other hand, a high school degree conveys little and the job market is considerably poorer. In order to achieve the post-secondary education usually needed for economic success, today's young guns have incurred historic levels of student loan debt, often displacing the household budget-line traditionally earmarked for rent or a mortgage.

I could rant for pages on the idiocy of federal student loan policies, which are rapidly inflating college tuition rates—but I shall spare you. Suffice it to say this is a small tragedy. Members of the graduating class of 2013 averaged more than $35,000 in college-related debt. At an interest rate of 6.8 percent, that's more than $400 per month on a 10-year repayment schedule—more than a car payment, half-a-month's rent, or a month of groceries. Worse still, after realizing the size of the debt they incurred, nearly 40 percent of 2013 graduates said they wish they had done things differently. Nonetheless, having incurred the debt, half say that paying it off is a top financial priority—possibly explaining the decision to stay at home and postpone major life decisions, such as buying a new place or getting married.[36]

Here's the snare in which many Millennials are caught: In 2013, privately held student loan debt rocketed past $1 trillion. That's higher than the nation's credit card debt and it's almost certainly a bubble. Just as Washington precipitated the 2008-housing crisis by gobbling up private mortgages and offering perverse incentives for lenders to shell out loans to unqualified buyers, the feds have stimulated enormous demand for college enrollment. While the availability of government loans made college more accessible, it also disconnected the buyer (our ambitious young Millennial) from the cost of the product (a college education). Knowing that students can access bottomless bags of money (in the form of federal loans) to obtain Interpretive Dance degrees, and knowing that these loans create new demand for post-secondary education, colleges are free to hike tuition rates far faster than inflation. As a result, the cost of a four-year public institution has soared 357 percent in the past thirty years.[37] Essentially, young Millennials could buy a product with little regard for its cost. And colleges could sell a product with little regard for what students could actually afford.

Thanks, Uncle Sam.

Here's the bottom line: Barack Obama has presided over the slowest economic recovery since the Great Depression. As a result, the rate of family formation has slowed to levels not seen since—you guessed it—the Great Depression. That is why, at first, Millennials behaved no differently than prior generations when it came to shacking up with mom and dad. It was not until the onset of the Great Recession that the percentage of young adults living with their parents crept up by 4 percent, exceeding recent, post-War historical norms.[38]

Like their Depression-era grandparents and great-grandparents, Millennials appear to be reacting to economic pressures, not personal preferences. Indeed, most Millennials *want* to grow up, move out, and get on with their lives. They're not rejecting the American Dream—they are delaying it, and not by choice.

That's why 82 percent of young Americans say owning a home is important—more than any other generation. That number ticks up to 90 percent among married Millennials. [39] Surprisingly, most of them are eyeing a house in the suburbs, not downtown. The fact that many Millennials live in an urban area appears to be a matter of economics, not personal preference. Moreover, once married, Millennials prefer single-family homes to condos, apartments, or lofts. Among married Millennials, almost none live with their parents—and roughly half own a home. Put another way, once they are financially stable enough to get married, Millennials do what most prior generations have done: Settle down and live in the burbs.[40]

There is ample evidence this suburbanizing trend will continue. In the early 1970s, roughly 38 percent of Americans lived in the suburbs, compared to about 45 percent in 1980 and more than half in 2000. Today, suburban growth still outpaces that of the downtown core.[41] Millennials seem poised to continue on this path, with three times as many saying they prefer the suburbs to downtown. [42] However, unlike Boomers and Generation Xers, Millennials often settle close to their parents upon moving out or getting married. That's consistent with the finding that they tend to have good relationships with their parents and, typically, wish to live as they do. [43]

It's true that cohabitation and out-of-wedlock births are higher among Millennials. The latter, in particular, poses a very serious social problem and several attendant economic problems. Nevertheless, this appears to be a cross-generational concern. Roughly as many Millennials as Gen-Xers, Boomers, and Silents consider the rising share of single-parent households troubling.[44]

And it's not quite Sodom and Gomorrah out there either.

Teen drinking, smoking, pregnancies, violent crime and incarceration rates are all down dramatically over the past several decades. Some of these social ills have even reached all-time lows.[45] And while weddings have grown somewhat less common, some 70 percent of unmarried Millennials still say they want to get married and the majority of those remaining say they're not yet sure. When asked about their priorities, 52 percent of Millennials cite "Being a good parent," which topped the list. "Having a successful marriage" was in second place, followed by "Helping others in need" and "Owning a home" at 21 and 20 percent, respectively. "Becoming famous" ranked last, at 1 percent. When it comes to valuing good parenting, Millennials edge out the general population by two points. That's particularly surprising when you consider that only 34 percent of Millennials have had children yet.[46]

Without a doubt, the Great Recession and the jobless "recovery" that followed has been a difficult economic experience for everyone. However, for Millennials, it has also been the *only* economic experience. And that leads me to the third key factor shaping Millennials' culture and outlook: Expectations.

While we remain more optimistic than prior generations, the Great Recession has cast our high expectations in stark relief. Not since the 1920s has the harsh reality of recession collided so spectacularly with lofty expectations.

To illustrate, let me introduce you to Jonny. He's a Millennial.

Raised on ample doses of self-esteem and fed a steady supply of participation trophies, Jonny grew up feeling rather special. Though he's a chronic underachiever, Jonny gets plenty of accolades from mom and dad, who seek to raise him in a household more nurturing than the one in which they were raised.

The constant insistence that Jonny was special, that he was

destined for success and happiness did not create entitlement, per se. Instead, it lifted Jonny's expectation of life and work, fostered the notion that anything was within reach and opened the door to expectation's close cousin, *ambition.*

Jonny doesn't just want a *good* job. He wants a *meaningful* job.

I know, you just threw up a little bit. After all, *everyone* wants a meaningful job. However, not every generation has insisted on meaningful work as a precondition of personal happiness. But that's the Millennial. For them, the search for fulfillment may manifest in a number of ways: More frequent job-hopping, higher rates of extracurricular community service, and the widely-observed inclination among entrepreneurial Millennials to seek greater control over their companies, instead of simply cashing out and buying a boat.

Put simply, many Millennials were told they were special. And many believed it.

Enter, reality.

In school, Jonny's parents told him he was a stellar musician, artist, basketball player, and debate champion—but he figured out they were wrong when he couldn't play the right note, paint a decent picture, nail a free throw, or win an argument.

For Jonny, high school was where a lot of dreams collided with reality.

But not *every* dream. It's easier for someone to buy into the notion that, while they may not have any apparently standout qualities, they possess something indefinable that destines them for happy, meaningful work. That's Jonny.

Raised on high expectations, he is soon crushed by the realization that employer after employer is not hiring; that 16 years of schooling has not adequately prepared him to get a good job, let alone a *meaningful* one; that *under*employment is a distinct, sobering possibility.

Jonny's parents didn't have this problem for two reasons: First, economic conditions were better when they entered the workforce. Second, their expectations were never so high as Jonny's. Of course, they wanted good jobs. But work was *work.* It wasn't necessarily a crusade or even a passion.

Like those before them, Jonny's parents anticipated that they would outdo the prior generation. After all, that's how America worked. Subsequently, when Jonny's parents rode the Reagan-wave and surpassed their parents, they were happy. Their expectations were exceeded.

Naturally, Jonny thought he'd do better than mom and dad, too.

He hit the books, went to college, racked up a ton of a debt, and entered the workforce—only to find a much tougher economic environment than he'd imagined. His expectations were unmet.

One of those new-fangled Internet blogs, *Wait Buy Why*, has a simple equation that elegantly sums up the whole thing:

Happiness = Reality – Expectations

According to the author, "it's pretty straightforward—when the reality of someone's life is better than they had expected, they're happy. When reality turns out to be worse than the expectations, they're unhappy." Not surprisingly, an analysis of English-language print reveals that terms like "secure career" have declined dramatically in recent years, while terms like "follow your passion" have taken off in the last two decades—another indication that Millennials view work rather differently than prior generations. [47]

If our dreams had an epitaph, it would read, "Expected more than most. Ended up with less. Kinda sad about that." Either that or, "Oops, we elected the wrong guy."

The Millennial's outsized expectation of work can be extremely irritating to other generations. Hell, it's irritating to me. After all, *no one* craves an unsatisfying job—and *no one* has a *right* to a dream job either. Nonetheless, understanding these expectations is essential to understanding Millennials' culture and politics.

For Millennials, the Great Recession has been a social, political and economic blender of unmet expectations. Despite their stubborn optimism, young Americans entered a world in which jobs were difficult to find and seldom fulfilling. Politics was not the panacea that one charismatic leader promised. College generated enormous debt, but did not prove a one-way ticket to career fulfillment or wealth. Big institutions failed and yet no one seemed to have a better idea.

Turns out that hope and change never really materialized—or if they did, they sucked.

Ah, the politics of the Millennial. Tangled, confused, at once liberal and libertarian—pro-government yet, somehow, profoundly distrustful of government's ham-fisted handiwork; yet another wasteland of fizzled dreams and ideological tension.

Millennials' political engagement began with opposition to the foreign policy of the Bush administration. It reached its zenith in 2008 when Barack Obama appeared on the national stage as if a figment of the Millennial mind: Young, tech-savvy, casual, charismatic, and culturally modern. Forget politics, Obama was a celebrity.

Certainly, people in general—not just young people—gravitate to candidates who embody their ideal personal qualities. It's simply that Barack Obama's personality seemed to more closely approximate the Millennial ideal than it did for other age groups.

Candidate Obama was to Millennials what Candidate Reagan was to Boomers and what Candidate Kennedy was to Silents. He was a cultural phenomenon and his candidacy electrified a generation. Voting for Obama was not simply a political statement, it was a declaration of hope—it made people *feel good* about *themselves*. And that's why he won Millennials by 34 percent in 2008.

By 2012, *Candidate* Obama was gone and *President* Obama was left to grapple with the fact that things still pretty much sucked. However, the president's campaign team shrewdly shifted the debate from economic issues, to deal-breaking social matters with generational fault lines (a la the "War on Women" and "Same-Sex Marriage"), aimed at depicting Mitt Romney as a narrow-minded, knuckle-dragging Neanderthal.

At the same time, Obama cleverly portrayed the good Governor as a vulture capitalist—a man who understood the economy but had no intention of shaping it to the benefit of ordinary Americans and certainly not those lowest on the economic totem poll, such as Millennials. *He may be a good president for people like him, but not people like you,* suggested Obama. Although crass, Democrat efforts to render Mitt Romney an unacceptable alternative were effective.

In a sea of statistics, one stands out: When voters were asked which candidate "cares about people" like them, 81 percent named Obama. Only 18 percent named Romney. And that was the ballgame.

What made Millennials susceptible to Obama's charms—twice?

Well, the incumbent is almost always the default choice. Before tossing out the incumbent, voters look for proof that the alternative is acceptable. Everyone has heard the phrase: "The devil you know is better than the devil you don't." It applies here. The job of the challenger is to make himself a known quantity; to demonstrate that he is a viable alternative when it comes to handling the matters voters consider most important. To help them assess the qualities of the challenger, the Gen-Xer, the Boomer and the Silent are all able to recall successful past presidencies. They can more readily disqualify incumbents on the basis of incompetence—after all, they can remember a time when more capable leaders governed.

The Silent has been through "transformational" presidencies before—he's not as easily swayed by Barack Obama's "hope and change" platitudes. The Boomer remembers the successful leadership of Ronald Reagan—she knows a recovery should be well underway. The Gen-Xer recalls the centrist approach of Bill Clinton—he understands that presidents must occasionally cooperate with their political opponents to achieve lasting policy success.

However, when Mitt Romney declared he was a "conservative," Millennials thought of the only other self-described conservative president they could remember: George W. Bush. Unfortunately, the political frame of reference for the Millennial is largely limited to George W. Bush and Barack Obama, two presidencies that are widely considered less than stellar. In 2012, with this narrow frame of reference, the Millennial instinctively compared Obama with Bush— and tilted toward Obama.

Since then, a lot has changed.

Millennials have started to sour on government and drift rightward on economic policy. They still lean left on social matters—and probably always will. Compared to prior generations, they are less likely to consider themselves religious, less likely to believe the Bible should be taken literally, and more likely to support same-sex marriage. However, even many self-identified "liberal" Millennials will find well-articulated conservative economic populism appealing, particularly in the aftermath of an 8-year Obama presidency.

"There is a libertarian streak that is apparent among [...] left-of-center young people," the *Pew Center's* Andrew Kohut explained to *The New York Times'* Thomas Edsall. "Socially liberal but very wary of government. Why? They came of age in an anti-government era when government doesn't work."[48]

Sure, Millennials are more likely to label themselves liberals. But that's only because their political identities tend to be based on social, rather than economic issues—at least for the moment. On economic matters, however, even liberal Millennials are starting to sound pretty damn conservative by most measures.

For example, while 73 percent of older self-identified liberals say, "government should do more to solve problems," only 44 percent of younger self-identified liberals agree. Instead, most believe, "government is trying to do too much." Again, these are *left-leaning* young voters—not Millennials as a whole. Similarly, older liberals are far more likely than their younger counterparts to blame poverty on circumstances, say Wall Street hurts the economy, or believe government should do more to help the needy, even if it means more debt. By contrast, strong majorities of young liberals say government can't afford a bigger social safety net and that "Wall Street helps the American economy more than it hurts."[49]

On some issues, the gulf between older, more traditional liberals and younger self-styled "liberals" is truly enormous.

Pew found that fully 80 percent of older liberals believe "racial discrimination is the main reason why many blacks can't get ahead." Only 19 percent of younger liberals agreed. Similarly, 91 percent of old schoolers felt the "US needs to continue making changes to give blacks equal rights," while a mere 28 percent of young liberals agreed.[50] This is the sort of divide you would expect to find between political parties, not like-minded voters of different ages. However, these trends are merely symptoms of "the most striking social, racial, and economic shifts the country has seen in a century," notes *Pew*.[51]

After 2012, Democrats think they have Millennials in the bag. They don't.

Compared to prior generations, Millennials are less likely to define themselves according to political party, more likely to cross party lines, and more likely to consider themselves *Independents*— making them easier to sway. While this generation leans left on social matters, it will be increasingly up for grabs in the coming decades, as their simmering economic instincts are brought to a boil.

For conservatives, successfully contesting this age group is not optional—it is *essential.* Whether or not America fails depends in large part upon whether or not it abandons the Left's terrible political software and renews an age-old commitment to individualism, entrepreneurship, and free market innovation. If Millennials embrace these values—as they seem inclined to do— conservatism will enjoy a new renaissance. If not, it will wither on the vine. As a result, unlocking the code to the Millennial's political DNA is an essential part of a second American century.

Right now, that seems like one hell of a tall order. After all, we look like Generation Contradiction.

We no longer believe government can fix our lives or our problems, but we tend to vote for more of it. We're derided as technology-addled narcissists, but we manage to score high on volunteerism and community-mindedness. We're distrustful of traditional institutions and hierarchies, but we are known as rule-followers who often relate well to our parents. Millennial's say they want to be rich more than any other generation, but we are credited with fomenting the Occupy Wall Street movement. We've piled up mountains of student loan debt, but we've become far more frugal than our parents. Surveys suggest we may be averse to hard work, but we're intensely entrepreneurial. Many of us are urban dwellers, who'd rather live in suburbia. We have more formal education than any other generation, but may face a tougher path to prosperity.

Most of all, Millennials despise hypocrisy yet seem to embody clear contradictions.

But maybe these aren't contradictions at all. Maybe it's a case of culture clashing with politics, expectations colliding with reality, hope crashing into change. I think these conflicts represent the tension between our generation's underlying culture and its overlying politics, which will be resolved as we mature. As this tension is resolved, our politics will evolve to more fully reflect our generational culture.

In recent years, Millennials have endured more than the standard dosage of intergenerational faultfinding, thanks to a super-connected world in which every opinion has an outlet. However, this information overload has popularized a number of misconceptions (or at least, misinterpretations) about these young Americans, such as: They're lazy, feckless Peter Pans; narcissistic, tech-crazed dunces addicted to seemingly-bottomless barrels of parental charity; hapless devotees of a hopeless hookup culture with no intention of ever settling down or starting a family; overeducated underachievers more interested in socializing online, playing video games, and indulging infantile self-fulfillment fantasies than growing up, moving out, and getting a job.[52]

There are plenty of stories out there that seem to back it up—we hear them all the time. The young job applicant who brings his mother with him to an interview; the overconfident meathead with the popped collar who asks for a raise and a promotion within the first few weeks of a new gig; the 20-something food stamp recipient who glorifies laziness—the list goes on and on. Unfortunately, technology has handed a megaphone to some of my generation's biggest morons.

So, to Millennials: If you're a 32 year-old parental basement dweller with a Russian Lit degree chasing Peter Pan fantasies, *get your shit together.* Your parents may tolerate your pointless, never-ending journey toward self-actualization—which looks a lot like eating hot pockets and playing Minecraft all day—but, seriously, you're giving the rest of us a bad name. No one owes you a dream or even a job. The sooner you figure that out, the sooner you'll have a shot at both.

And, to Boomers: Fans of the ever-popular, always-cantankerous "get off my lawn" genre of mainstream opinion-journalism will ruefully recall that Boomers were once widely panned as the laziest of generations—by *their* parents. Then and now, such characterizations are a better reflection of intergenerational grousing than genuine no-goodness. "Part of the problem," writes the *Boston Daily's* Eric Randall, "is that the grumps at America's magazines and newspapers do not have the ability to wait and see. No, they must declare a generation of people currently aged 13 to 30 total failures *today*."[53] There is little doubt that working hard, achieving success, and grimly doubting the ability of the next generation to do the same is part of a long-standing American tradition. However, we cannot let this time-honored ritual of lambasting the ne'er do-wells behind us to become an actual, operable, worldview.

Since the dawn of recorded time, stern-faced elders have been grumbling about the no-goodniks farther down the generational totem pole. "You can find these complaints in ancient Greek literature, in the Bible," Peter Cappelli, director of the Center for Human Resources at the *Wharton School*, tells *The New York Times*. "It reflects the way old people see young people," says Cappelli, who notes that youth attitudes toward work are little changed since Boomers scared the shit out of *their* parents way back in the 60s.[54]

Sure, it's easy to draw *big* conclusions based on *small* examples, to allow anecdotes to stand in for data. But we *want* data. There's already enough unfounded, disconnected drivel out there. So, as much as possible, I'm going to stick with the science. Whenever feasible, I'm going to rely on survey data, focus group research, scientific study, and economic indicators to paint a picture. I hope that the resulting picture is more accurate than the casual conclusions drawn from a handful of personal encounters.

Millennials are growing up. By the 2030s, they will begin to inherit the reigns of America's major corporate, political, and social institutions. Things will look different—but they won't look bad. Emerging from a decade of economic and political difficulty, Millennials will power a *Great Transition* that finally drags government into the Information Age and sets the stage for a mid-century *Turning Point* that will inaugurate a new era of American prosperity.

THE GREAT TRANSITION

CHAPTER 3
MILLENNIALS & MONEY

If they're not quite tightwads, Millennials are at least devout penny-pinchers.

Don't believe me? You're in the majority. Given the popular depiction of Millennials as brand-obsessed, budget-busting materialists, it's no shock that 53 percent of older Americans think younger generations will turn out less financially disciplined than their predecessors.[55]

If not for the last six years, they might very well have been right.

Yet, the last six years *did* happen. And after watching their parents struggle financially and wrestle with a difficult job market themselves, Millennials are actually "a lot more disciplined," explains Alok Prasad, head of the online investing firm, *Merrill Edge*. They tend to be financially cautious and uncommonly self-controlled, namely "in terms of thinking ahead, and being proactive about saving for the future."[56] Perhaps as a result, young Americans tend to be more frugal shoppers, less brand-conscious, and less brand-loyal than Baby Boomers and Gen-Xers. In fact, studies by the banking industry show the Great Recession has shaped Millennials' financial habits, much as the Great Depression shaped the habits of their grandparents and great-grandparents.[57]

The common misconception that Millennials are debt-crazy misses the mark, points out Anisha Sekar, an analyst with the personal finance website, *NerdWallet*. The group's recent study on the financial habits of Millennials indicates the vast majority of their debt is tied to education, not credit card spending.[58]

"Younger folk have lower credit card debt than any other age cohort," she notes. "That shows they are able to distinguish between an investment and a consumption purchase. Millennials aren't as willing to go into debt for short-term gain, but they are willing to go into debt for a long-term investment such as education." [59]

By the time Millennials joined the workforce the economy was tanking, government spending was soaring, and pension plans had become scarce (at least outside of government). Buffeted by these *three headwinds*, young Americans found themselves muddling through the toughest economy since the Great Depression.

The first headwind: The Great Recession left many Boomers scrambling to shore up depleted retirement savings—but it also left their Millennial children struggling to find entry level work as companies cut back and Boomers delayed retirement.

The second headwind: The Great Recession triggered massive government spending. Revenue plummeted. Deficits soared. Social Security began paying out more than it took in. Tens of trillions in unfunded liabilities led more than half of young Americans to conclude that the entitlement programs built by previous generations would become insolvent long before Millennials would ever use them.

The third headwind: Defined benefit plans are little more than folklore to most Millennials. Relics of the post-War industrial boom, pensions belonged to our grandparents and perhaps our parents. Almost none will belong to us. The private sector has already shed most of its defined benefit plans. With many Millennials working as part-timers, contractors, or small business owners, we consider ourselves lucky to find a company with a 401k matching plan.

The result: It's on us—and we know it.

Surveys indicate that most Millennials expect neither private pensions nor Social Security. Since we frequently found traditional employment avenues closed, we are uncommonly eager to freelance, moonlight, or start our own companies. Our propensity to take on "side-gigs" is largely a product of economic fear and insecurity. Studies show that, compared to our parents, we are more frugal, more apt to budget, more interested in starting a business, and more likely to invest in our retirement while still young. Consequently, the average Millennial began saving for retirement at age 22. The average Boomer, age 35.[60] [61]

Wait a second. Aren't Millennials dragging around more than a trillion dollars in college-related student loan debt? Yes, *and they know it.* In fact, paying off that debt is a top priority of most Millennials who've had the misfortune of incurring it. Like the Sword of Damocles, that debt dangles over Millennials' heads, driving them to become cautious, conservative investors, and even more assiduous savers.

Economically, we're similar to our grandparents. But politically, the similarities are quickly shrinking.

The countless hardships of the Great Depression drove our grandparents to embrace FDR's New Deal and the promise of government-granted economic security. That decision gave rise to the welfare state. At first, Millennials walked a similar path. The onset of the Great Recession juiced Millennial support for Barack Obama, who spoke shamelessly of "spreading the wealth around." To many jobless, pension-less undergrads the guarantee of *economic security* was more enticing than the chance for *economic opportunity*. However, where FDR strengthened liberalism's brand, Obama has tarnished it. His presidency seems destined to create more long-term skeptics than converts.

The lesson to young Americans: Government can't solve big problems.

A lot of Millennials didn't know that. But, they learned it—the hard way. Now, poll after poll shows young voters have lost faith in the president they twice elected and the government they eagerly empowered. Stumbling through the sixth year of Barack Obama's "recovery," countless Millennials find themselves cracking their thirties unmarried, underemployed, and unexpectedly *hopeless.*

Obama had a shot at his FDR moment. He blew it. Instead of proving Washington smart, nimble and capable, he proved it to be the dinosaur it truly is—antiquated, unwieldy, and stupid. Obamacare anyone?

With their support for public institutions plummeting, their faith in elected leaders vanishing, and their trust in the problem-solving power of government reaching all-time lows, penny-pinching Millennials turned elsewhere.

The result? Government is out. Startups are in.

More than half of Millennials own or aim to start a business within the next two years, outstripping the general population by 10 percent.[62] [63] Still trapped in the wake of the Great Recession, much of that entrepreneurial energy is pent-up, locked-down. It will take a true economic recovery to release it, to return *economic opportunity*, rather than *security*, to the position of *chief economic value.* Sure, plenty of young office flunkies won't escape the corporate grind to launch a startup—but many will. Even if entrepreneurship doesn't take off in the post-Obama years, this generation's startup dreams seem awfully enterprising for a bunch typically considered hostile to capitalism.

Call me an optimist, but I think entrepreneurship *will* take off— that a new age of free enterprise is within sight. Not because of government, but in spite of it. The free market is more resilient than we give it credit. Take energy, for example. Despite the determined efforts of this administration to snuff out the oil and natural gas industries, they have thrived. In fact, these industries not only single-handedly drove job-growth during the Great Recession—they catapulted the United States to the top of the energy heap.

Ham-handed regulations have, tragically, closed the door to some entrepreneurial ventures. However, technology has flung open countless windows to others. It's dramatically reduced the entry barrier for entrepreneurs, allowing flexible work hours and flexible geography. It's reducing the time and capital required to move ideas into the marketplace and made it easier, from a practical standpoint, to form a company. At the same time, it's made investment capital more fluid and accessible. Technology has also made relationships—personal and professional—that heretofore would have been impossible, simple.

Millennials are "enthusiastic about entrepreneurship, and that is good news for the US," says Carl Schramm, president and CEO of the Kauffman Foundation, "They recognize that entrepreneurship is the key to reviving the economy."[64] They also recognize that today's world comes with fewer guarantees. These days, starting a business seldom means forgoing a pension—you weren't going to get one anyway. It seldom means forgoing a stable, long-term union job—there aren't many of those around anymore. So, the opportunity-cost of small business ownership is down—and that's good. It means greater *Economic Dynamism*—more innovation and more creative destruction.

Two thousand years ago, the economy of the Roman Empire was powered by conquest. Today, the American economy is powered by creative destruction, the combustible process whereby new products, services, and ideas replace old ones. This sort of entrepreneurship fuels *Economic Dynamism*—perhaps the most important of the *Five Pillars of American Power*. *Economic Dynamism* drives productivity and growth, which in turn funds the national defense and supports the military and diplomatic infrastructure that makes global free trade—and the entire American-led international order—possible.

However, for Millennials, entrepreneurship isn't just economically desirable—it's culturally celebrated. While Wall Streeters are reviled, small business owners and tech giants are revered. Millennials watched as companies like Google, Facebook, PayPal, and others went from small startups to titanic, publicly traded companies. They watched as government flailed about helplessly, careening from one crisis to the next, while private sector entrepreneurs pioneered new industries and new ideas. Hell, at the same time Washington was neutering America's space program, young Americans witnessed enterprising billionaires launch their own. Silicon Valley startups may be a dime a dozen, but the entrepreneurship instinct it embodies has seeped into every aspect of Millennial culture.

As a result, the most prosperous Millennials tend to invest in themselves. Adam Nash, Chief Operating Officer at *Wealthfront* notes that, "the whole idea from the 80s—that you'd make some money and use that money to make more money—this current generation isn't looking at money that way. The typical software engineer isn't dreaming of the day he can quit the rat race. They use their money instead to gain a little bit of control over what they work on and what they do."[65]

Most of us owe that instinct to our parents.

They told us we could do anything—and we believed them. Sure, that's led to many unhappy collisions between expectations and reality. However, sometimes expectations *shape* reality. And *that* has created some of my generation's most brilliant entrepreneurs, who formed intensely dynamic companies already changing the world. These entrepreneurs are doing what they love. They don't want to stop; they want to do more, to obtain greater control over their professional passions.

It makes perfect sense and it's also likely to be the case with the many Millennials forced to delay their dreams. In pursuit of their passion, they often incurred enormous student loan debt, found the job market in shambles, settled for any gig they could find, bottled up their dreams, and put them on the shelf, waiting.

Once the economy recovers from eight years of Obama-induced stupor, many of those bottled up dreams—much of that simmering entrepreneurial urge—will finally burst out into the marketplace. Buoyed by easy access to technology, expect the number of freelancers, independent contractors, and small business owners to grow. This will strengthen America's *Economic Dynamism.*

It's fitting that the rise of this new bootstrap meritocracy will coincide with the death knell of enforced mediocrity: Unions.

In the 1950s, more than a third of the workforce was unionized. Today, it's little more than a tenth and falling. The United Auto Workers (UAW)—one of the country's oldest and most politically influential unions—has seen its membership crater from 1.5 million in 1979 to less than 400,000 in 2012.[66] In what's been dubbed the UAW's *Waterloo*, union bosses failed to unionize a Volkswagen plant in Tennessee, despite a cooperative employer, favorable scheduling, and full access to the company's employees. Even under these uniquely advantageous conditions, unions were unable to win majority support from the plant's workers.[67]

This trend will continue.

"Capital is mobile," writes George Will. "It goes where it is welcomed and stays where it is well treated," which is why most plants recently constructed by foreign automakers are located in the South. As courageous governors end the corrupt practice of forcibly shoveling taxpayer money into union coffers, public sector unions will continue to decline, too. The fall of unions and the renaissance of entrepreneurship will create new economic and political realities.[68] [69]

Millennials will ride the crest of this wave.

And just as Millennials assume the reigns of America's top companies and institutions, we'll fully realize what Thomas Friedman calls "the 401(k) world." It's a world in which conservatives should thrive, in which the entrepreneurial and the innovative will go farther and get there faster than ever before:

What's exciting is that this platform empowers individuals to access learning, retrain, engage in commerce, seek or advertise a job, invent, invest and crowd source — all online. But this huge expansion in an individual's ability to do all these things comes with one big difference: more now rests on you.

If you are self-motivated, wow, this world is tailored for you. The boundaries are all gone. But if you're not self-motivated, this world will be a challenge because the walls, ceilings, and floors that protected people are also disappearing. That is what I mean when I say "it is a 401(k) world." Government will do less for you. Companies will do less for you. Unions can do less for you. There will be fewer limits, but also fewer guarantees. Your specific contribution will define your specific benefits much more. Just showing up will not cut it. [70]

For all the recent uproar over income inequality, we're talking about the triumph of meritocracy over mediocrity. After a long hiatus, an age-old American promise is poised to make a comeback: You can rise as far as your talent will take you.

For self-starters, this is glorious stuff.

It means a new model of work that elevates talent and innovation, rather than seniority and clock punching. It means that impediments to innovation will crumble and new pathways to progress will open. For a while, government will thrash about wildly—shoveling a mess of subsidies to flagging industries and tossing crony capitalist-style "incentives" to others. Likewise, the Left will attempt to squeeze more time out of the aging entitlement model by dodging reform as long as possible. Indeed, liberals have already revived tired old arguments about income inequality.

Yet, rising income inequality is not necessarily a fixture of the future, nor is it necessarily a barrier to social mobility. After all, income inequality soared after the American Revolution and again during the pre-Depression "Gilded Age." Both periods were times of transition, just as now, and both were temporary.[71]

No matter what, I'm quite certain that making your neighbor poorer will not make you richer. That's why I'm not interested in income inequality; I'm interested in social mobility. Too often, the Left conflates the two. Sure, you'd have plenty of social mobility if the richest guy around only earned $50,000 a year—because it's easier to go from $25,000 to $50,000 than it is to go from $25,000 to, say, a $1 million. The liberal doesn't see the difference. But the true conservative knows social mobility should be about improving the standard of living for everyone—not yelling at people who live in big houses.

Fortunately, Tom Friedman's emerging "401(k) world" is built for social mobility.

Here's what we are leaving behind: A defined benefits world of tenures and unions, limited risk but limited opportunity. Here's what is taking shape: A defined contributions world of merit pay and worker choice—a dynamic world that elevates those with the talents to rise; a world in which you get out what you put in. [72]

Do liberals really believe that this world will belong to them?

Do they believe that Millennials—with their 401ks, frugal spending habits, entrepreneurial DNA, and distaste for all things big—will stick with the party that stands for platinum-plated government pensions, soaring deficits, bloated bureaucracies, and centralized power *forever?*

A generation filled with frugal entrepreneurs and disciplined savers, with little faith in federal lifelines, will not forever tolerate deficit spending—particularly now that the Obama presidency is unraveling. As Millennials obtain more economic responsibility and as the GOP inevitably moderates its position on same-sex marriage, Democrats will have an even tougher time hoodwinking these voters.

A generation forced to embrace entrepreneurship; to pursue economic risk because economic security was not available—a generation that does not believe it can depend on government for retirement but, instead, must depend on itself, will not long tolerate an entitlement system that borders on bankruptcy. At the moment, the Millennial's frugality is a purely cultural (rather than political) feature. However, these miserly instincts are part of the genes of our generation. As I'll cover in later chapters, experience will force these genes to manifest; our culture will begin to drive our politics.

In this way, the Millennial's fiscal prudence will strengthen *Domestic Stability*, one of the *Five Pillars of American Power*. Though excessive saving can be an economic albatross, Washington will generally benefit from the parsimonious, recession-forged instincts of today's young Americans. Indeed, surveys indicate Millennials are far more inclined to trim entitlement spending, reduce benefits, and favor private Social Security accounts than previous generations. By the 2020s, the Millennial's politically against-type support for entitlement reform will make it tougher for liberals to assail the conservative position, finally opening the door to meaningful reform and setting the stage for a mid-century *Turning Point.*

Of course, Democrats think Republicans are relics. And they're right.

But Democrats are relics, too—they just don't know it. As I'll discuss later, both partisan labels have lost their luster, for good or bad. Yet, the core economic tenets of conservatism are ideally suited to 21st Century values. Consider: Conservatives do not support bigger bureaucracies. We do not support bigger labor unions. We do not support crony capitalism. We do not support insolvent entitlement programs. We do not support concentrating power in Washington. We support *individuals* and their natural right to pursue happiness, however they see fit. *That* is the ethos of the new age.

Building on these emerging advantages, smart conservative candidates will eventually rehabilitate our brand, just as Reagan did in the 1980s. It may happen in 2016. It may not.

But, inevitably, it *will* happen.

When it does, conservatives will run on their ideas. What will liberals do?

CHAPTER 4
MILLENNIALS & THE MEDIA

When I don't love technology, I really hate it.

It's accelerated the already-frenetic pace of news, magnifying tales of human misery, corruption and malice—creating the commonly held (and tragically inaccurate) belief that our problems are bigger than our brains, that the end is neigh, that we're *screwed*.

But let's not bury ourselves yet.

Severe famine, rampant disease, widespread poverty, and endless bloodshed are the hallmarks of human history, at least most of it. Yet, there can be little doubt that modern life is characterized by considerably less violence, less misery, less hunger, and greater prosperity than any previous era in human history.

For some, that may be hard to believe. After all, it doesn't *feel* like we dwell at the peak of human progress. With scenes of violence, poverty, and oppression—not to mention rank stupidity—beamed straight to our flat-screens, we routinely ask, "What is the world coming to?" Round-the-clock coverage of mass killings, major trials, political gridlock, or public scandals create the impression that life is getting *worse*. Yet, this is merely one of technology's tricks: Rapid progress has now made it possible for us to *doubt* progress on a much grander scale.

My parents weren't raised in this feverish, chaotic media climate. I was. For me, there was no learning curve because there was nothing to *unlearn*. I never grew accustomed to print media. I don't think I've ever watched the 6 o'clock news—most of my reading is done online—and I've never owned a phone without a camera. This strange, spastic media ecosystem is, for better or worse, my natural habitat.

It's why "Millennials are always on," explains Anna Kassoway,

Chief Marketing Officer at social influencing platform, *Crowdtap*. Her firm's study on how young Americans interact with various forms of media reveals that the typical 18 to 36 year old spends an astounding 18 hours per day consuming or engaging with media—everything from texting to television. *Many of these hours overlap.* For example, what I'm doing at this very moment: Furiously composing my magnum opus while flipping between various news articles, periodically firing back texts as the TV hums along pleasantly in the background.[73]

If it weren't so normal, it would be downright bizarre.

When strange-looking space aliens (excuse me, culturally diverse extraterrestrials) sift through the bones of our irradiated civilization thousands of years from now, our penchant for juggling so many media platforms simultaneously may be one of the few human oddities that fascinates them. Or maybe they won't give a damn.

Either way, you can blame two things for this frenzied, fast-paced media environment: Computers got smaller and the Internet went wireless. Soon, users demanded new content—entertainment, news, opinion—and lots of it. Of course, that meant more traditional media displayed in new formats. But here's the really interesting thing: Around 30 percent of Millennials' total daily media consumption is user-generated content, including photos, blogs, email, texts, and, of course, social media posts.[74]

User-generated content is tech-speak for "stuff not made by professionals." It encompasses everything from overlong Facebook diatribes and uncomfortably expressive travel reviews to thought-provoking blogs and, my favorite, controversial web-videos.

This user-generated media is—for better or worse—filling the space once occupied by traditional business, civic, and social institutions. Trust the government, the news media or the corporation? Nope. *Trust each other.* That's a core component of the Millennial's ethos. Rightly or wrongly, Millennials trust user-generated content 40 percent more than information purveyed by other media, including the news. That means checking *TripAdvisor* before going on vacation, consulting *Yelp* before dining out, and probably even scrolling through reader reviews before buying this book—and, importantly, valuing those user-reviews more highly than something read in *The New York Times*.[75]

Once in awhile, someone tells me this is a maturity thing—a *fad*.

But don't expect young Americans to suddenly swap out their smartphones for print newspapers when they get older. It's headed in the opposite direction. Recent years have shown a dramatic increase in the number of people who get most of their news from the Internet, with Millennials accounting for a big part of the jump. Nearly 60 percent now cite the Internet as a main news source, compared with 13 percent of Silents (those born during the Great Depression and World War II).

Moreover, this trend has crept its way up the generational totem pole, with significant percentages of Gen-Xers and Boomers now calling the Internet a main news source, too. At 65 percent, TV remains King of the Hill for Millennials and they are about as likely to get their news from the boob tube as other age groups—even though they're increasingly viewing TV programming on various mobile devices. As the barriers between mediums continue to erode, don't be surprised if TVs become computers and vice versa.[76]

Despite its irritating social side effects, this "tech-effect" has enabled *the Individual* to mount something of a comeback.

The days of practiced uniformity, typified by factory-style fashion, entertainment, news media, and even education are disintegrating. You don't have to watch the 6 o'clock network news anymore—take your pick of seemingly endless options and watch when you want, where you want. Tired of cable? Go binge watch on Netflix or Hulu. No time to fit a campus into your quest for a college degree? Try an online university. No luck getting published by a mainstream newspaper? Consider an online outlet—or start your own. Don't like nine of the ten songs in that album? Buy the one you really want on iTunes (that is, unless the fascists at the record label make you buy the whole damn thing).

Of course, all generations have adopted modern technology—from cell phones to social networks—to some extent. Indeed, Baby Boomers are largely responsible for laying the foundation of the Information Age with the invention and propagation of the personal computer. For Millennials, it is not technology, but rather the natural, seamless integration of technology into our daily lives that is most notable. It is the sense that technology is normal, rather than novel, that sets the Millennial apart.

The most important generational divide can be found in the expectation of the consumer, eh hem, *user*. Over the last 60 years in general, and the last 15 years in particular, uniformity has been on the decline and individualism has been on the rise. Millennials have grown up in an environment of unprecedented customization and choice, which is reflected in our increasingly fragmented popular culture.

Take fashion, for example. In the 1950s, it was post-military uniformity all the way: Pencil skirts and petticoats, cardigans and wet hair. The 1960s were known for upending the status quo of the

50s, embracing go-go boots, pillbox hats, and bowl-cuts. The 70s were all about hot pants, platform shoes, and bell-bottomed jeans. The 80s gave us power dressing and perms, close-fitting trousers and loose-fitting shirts, *Magnum, PI* mustaches and macho mullets. It was awful.

But by the late 90s, mainline fashion began to crumble—replaced by a growing desire for customization. From baggy pants to skinny jeans, style was all over the map by the turn of the millennium. Gone was the "signature look" of decades past, replaced by increasingly personalized and eclectic styles. Is it a byproduct of the Millennial's overconfidence and over-validation that they think they can attire themselves so diversely, so haphazardly even? Perhaps. These days, every high school seems to have "that guy who sports fedoras," or "that kid who wears clown shoes," or "that dude who insists on wearing purple knee socks" or something. But I think this has less to do with permissive parents and more to do with modern technology and the expectations it creates. We live in a "Build Your Own Playlist" world, based on a broader acceptance of diverse styles and greater insistence on individual preferences.

And almost any style has become acceptable—so long as it's *yours.*

And it's not just fashion. Today, the best brands celebrate choice and work hard to deliver it. Soft drink companies now sell a dizzying array of flavors—you can even mix your own. Technology firms promote app stores brimming with choices. Online travel agencies let you plan your fantasy vacation and even "name your own price."[77] Car companies struggle to make assembly lines nimble enough to build cars suited to every desire. It's customization for the common man, or as Britton Monasco writes, it's no longer about the supply side; it is now about the demand side.[78]

This tech-driven, choice-oriented ethos began with consumers. Marketers bottled and sold personal choice to young Millennials en masse, from iTunes to Netflix to SodaStream. Now, businesses are seeking to accommodate choice in the workplace, from flexible hours to flexible geography. Churches offer a range of services—not just various slots but numerous formats and a wide array of small groups catering to individual lifestyles and preferences. Love it or hate it (and you should love it), we're now free to exercise unprecedented levels of choice in every sphere of our lives—with the notable exception of backwards-ass government, which I will tackle in the next chapter.

So, Millennials are draped in personal technology, perpetually (and blissfully) connected, comfortable and accustomed to unlimited information, yet increasingly skeptical of the news outlets that traditionally supply it. What does this mean for media in the next few decades?

Fragmentation.

In the 60s, there were three major news networks and a handful of powerful print outlets. By the turn of the century, cable news had joined the fray, conservatives had built an empire in exile on talk radio, and a small band of Internet news-breakers had started hurling rocks at the establishment. Today, print news is collapsing. Internet news is expanding. TV and radio are evolving. Media conglomerates are consolidating at the same time audiences are fracturing. And Millennials are riding the crest of the wave.

Take it from John Kerry: "This little thing called the Internet [...] makes it much harder to govern."

Spoken like a true tin-pot tyrant, John. But he's right.

The Internet, nonstop cable news coverage, the ease of travel, mobile computing: These developments wire us to the world in a way that makes all of us, as consumers of information, very different from Americans living half a century ago. Now, every cellphone can become a video camera. Every injustice can become a social media event. Every email contains the potential for scandal. The Internet made it harder for government to, you know, *govern*. But it also personalized the creation and delivery of news—you can consume information when you want, where you want, in any medium you want, according to whatever political persuasion you want. Gone is the era of three-network dominance, where stone-faced anchors calmly delivered an hour's worth of hard news every day.

Millennials grew up in an entirely new media ecosystem.

It all started with the first Gulf War. CNN, the first cable news network, offered 24-hour coverage of the American-led effort to expel Saddam Hussein from Kuwait. Suddenly, ordinary Americans were connected to the war at all times of the day. By 2003, early-wave Millennials were starting to vote and Fox News was leading cable coverage of the Second Gulf War. Missiles lit up the night sky over Baghdad and Saddam's statue was toppled in Firdos Square— all on TV. Shortly thereafter, expansive Internet-based news, social media, and mobile devices would take this connectivity to another level. Led by guerrilla journalists, like Matt Drudge, an army of online bloggers, commentators, and reporters democratized the news and bypassed the old media. New stories and new angles first challenged and then, later, began to shape the national agenda.

At first, it seemed that Drudge was the lone conservative wolf in the digital space—single-handedly watchdogging traditional media outlets. Eventually, others jumped in. *Breitbart, The Blaze, HotAir, The Daily Caller, RedState*—they're leaders in a robust and growing conservative media space that's challenging the Left, organizing the Right, and *finally* speaking to younger voters, who are accustomed to alternative news outlets. These pioneer journalists and commentators are also riding technology's tailwind, breaking the Left's long-time news media monopoly. They're on the right side of history, using digital media to diffuse power and limit the influence of government, filling a role too often vacated by traditional vassals of the Fourth Estate.

With the power to shape the national debate, these insurgent journalists lifted new arguments out of obscurity and thrust them into the limelight. Though often a wasteland for ridiculous videos about cats and unicorns, YouTube—and other sharing platforms like it—remade home learning, information sharing and advertising. These enormous changes are all taking place in the private sector, moving content-creation into the hands of ordinary people and diffusing power, even as governments cling tighter to Industrial-era controls.

Fifteen years ago, viral videos like *If I Wanted America to Fail* would not have been possible. Not only would the video have been more difficult to create and share, it would have been overlooked by traditional, old school media outlets. It took a combination of talk radio, Twitter, online news, and cable news to make it a viral success. This type of fragmented media environment, fostered by technology and quite comfortable to most Millennials, only exists in a world where people have lots of *choices*. As a result, this unique environment favors the individual, not the state. It favors one-to-one relationships between peers, rather than top-down relationships between institutions and constituents. At the same time, it has become another powerful vehicle to distribute American culture and values—a key component of *Cultural Universalism,* one of the *Five Pillars of American Power.*

The tech-effect has profound implications for traditional institutions. Indeed, smart observers of different political backgrounds seem to recognize the extent to which modern technology is reshaping politics and media; returning power to users. "The devices and connectivity so essential to modern life put unprecedented power in the hands of every individual—a radical redistribution of power that our traditional institutions don't and perhaps can't understand," writes Nicco Mele, author of *The End of 'Big'.* Pollster Scott Rasmussen agrees, writing, "In America, power is decentralizing and individuals are being empowered. While the trend has been building for decades, the politicians are just starting to recognize it." [79]

This genie can't be stuffed back in the bottle.

It seems that disruptive technology emerges in exactly the same size at exactly the same speed as government's efforts to control it. For example, in response to economic and privacy concerns, small groups of people around the globe began bootstrapping their own private versions of the Internet, called "meshes." A mesh is typically comprised of loose-knit collections of Wi-Fi antennas that shuttle data about in much the same way as the Internet. However, unlike the Internet, a mesh is controlled by its users, not the government. It's limited in size, free of NSA snooping, and cannot be shut down.[80] I'm not peddling some libertarian utopia here. After all, it's highly unlikely local meshes will ever replace the Internet or that a global mesh could be reliably constructed. The example merely serves to illustrate the point: This technology cannot be controlled.

Technology is de-professionalizing the gathering and delivery of news. Major news outlets will find it even more difficult to monetize hard news in an age where people increasingly prefer commentary; tougher to break stories at a time when competition for breaking news is fierce; and harder to hold audiences in an era of diminishing brand loyalty.

However, one thing will remain the same: News will almost always be bad.

Sorry, it's just the way it goes. We're quick to chastise the media for bringing us the bad news and only the bad news. "Why don't you report the good news?" we ask. Of course, we forget that the media—new and old—caters to its customers. How many of us would tune in to find out that a plane safely landed? That a crime went uncommitted? That a scandal never happened? Even if contemporary news is no worse than it was in 1985, there is simply *so much more of it* today than there was a generation ago. On our phones, in our offices, during lunch, dinner, and so much of the space in between, we are exposed to a steady drip of (mostly negative) news coverage. To anyone who doubts the ability of mass media to shape public opinion, I would submit that we live in *Exhibit A*—a period of unprecedented peace typified by unprecedented anxiety. Whether this anxiety is justified, whether our planet is on the brink of a new global catastrophe, is unknown.

What is clear to me, however, is that it's generally good that technology has put new tools in the hands of ordinary people—tools that were once available only to so-called professionals. The tech-effect is flattening industries from film to computer programming and elevating those with the most talent, rather than the best connections. But perhaps most importantly, technology (and without knowing it, Millennials), are breaking the Left's monopoly on the media.

As I'll discuss in the *Turning Point*, the tech effect is already reshaping America's *Three Cultural Drivers*: Education, Entertainment, and the News Media—with major long-term implications for the country and our politics. Long considered bastions of liberalism, these entrenched institutions are already undergoing tremendous fragmentation and change. For conservatives, who have been underdogs in the media arena for two generations, *fragmentation* is all upside.

After all, the new world isn't about "Big Government." It's about "Big Individual."

CHAPTER 5
MILLENNIALS & GOVERNMENT

Tim Carney is a smart guy.

Writing for the *Washington Examiner,* he points out that there is a big difference between how conservatives and liberals describe public life. For liberals, he notes, public life exists only within the narrow confines of government; it is *synonymous* with government. "Government is the name we give to the things we choose to do together," they say.[81]

They're wrong.

Last Sunday, I went to church. Tomorrow, I'm having dinner with my family. On Monday, I'm going to the office. Thankfully, I'm not doing any of these things with my government—but I'm doing all of them "together," with other people. When I *do* interact with government, it tends to be at the local level, where my elected leaders are most responsive and public services most effective. My interaction with the federal government is largely limited to the wholly unpleasant business of running the TSA grope-gauntlet and filing my taxes. [82]

Government is the word we give to the things we *must* do together. *Community* is the word we give to the things we *choose* to do together. The recent IRS, NSA, and VA scandals prove there's no such thing as a kinder, gentler federal government. That's why the best governments tend to be small and local—closer to the people.

It's not that government is bad. It's that the world has changed in fundamental ways and government hasn't yet adapted.

Washington is too big, too monolithic; it cannot thoughtfully administer the countless, complex needs of the choice-oriented society that is emerging. Just look at the modern economic landscape; it's startup city out there. MySpace was the reigning social media champ for only a few short years before Facebook became King of the Hill. Not long after Research in Motion introduced its Blackberry, Apple released iPhone and gobbled up the smartphone market. Taxicab companies are battling market-driven alternatives, like Uber. Brick-and-mortar bookstores are clashing with Amazon. Even old guard automakers face increasing competition from unlikely upstarts, like Tesla Motors. Lately, even the upstarts are battling upstarts. Today, the best companies succeed only by constantly reinventing themselves. For the brand-fickle Millennial, this is perfectly fine—the Great Recession has turned her into a value-seeker and technology has made her impatient. Whether she knows it or not, she's grown perfectly comfortable with creative destruction.

Government, on the other hand, is not. The feds are finding it increasingly difficult to regulate this vast, ever-changing marketplace. And Washington's attempt to manage this evolving economy is not only virtually impossible, it's *so 1935*. Today's business climate is far more open, accessible and dynamic than the static environs of the mid-Twentieth Century. And the old school institutions that once regulated this landscape have suffered serious, systemic damage to their credibility.

Moreover, President Obama has not restored their credibility; he has depleted it.

Case-in-point: The administration evidently expected Millennials to flock to its new Obamacare marketplaces in huge numbers to buy health insurance. They seem genuinely surprised this did not happen—and *that* is astounding. Today's young Americans are not simply tech savvy; they're tech-snobs—utterly intolerant of the slightest tech-related dysfunction. Moreover, they are resistant to the very top-down controls needed for Obamacare to function. And that's going to be even more obvious when the next wave of cancellations and penalties go out. Unfortunately for the administration, Millennials are *also* needed for Obamacare to function. Without them, premiums within the government-run exchanges will rise, insurers will limit healthcare options for consumers, and people will be *pissed*.

Of course, technology created the conditions for Millennials to drift from old institutions. However, it was the Great Recession that supplied the impetus. Washington's failed economic engineering (see bailouts and Obamacare) paired with the NSA's snooping left Millennials thinking the old institutions must have been built to solve yesterday's problems. It is crucial for *Domestic Stability* that public institutions be credible; that they earn the trust of the people.

But big is dying. And these institutions are simply *too big* to be credible.

As a generation—and increasingly, as a culture—we no longer trust *big*. As an adjective, we don't like it in front of government or labor anymore than we like it in front of business. When the Great Recession hit, many Millennials were shut out of these mighty institutions. Since then, we've watched them fail to spark meaningful economic recovery or break the political stalemate. They appear impotent, or worse, corrupt.

That's why—even though Millennials' *economic* experiences more closely parallel those of their Depression-era grandparents (or great grandparents) than their Reagan-era parents—their *political* experiences are entirely different. Today, America's public institutions have inspired eyeball-rolling at best and deep disappointment at worst. However, during the Great Depression, Franklin Roosevelt's robust central government inspired widespread popular support. It even earned him an unprecedented third (and, subsequently, fourth) term.

That's why it is not surprising FDR was able to usher in a *Great Transition*—leading government from a 19th Century post-Civil War model to a factory-style Industrial model in the space of a single decade. By the end of the Second World War, the United States had fully adapted to the symmetrical, mass production challenges of the day—long after the private sector had completed the transition.

These days, we tend to overlook the fact that World War II represented the high tide of central planning in America. I'm not talking about the introduction of Social Security. I'm referring to rationed food, medicine, materials, price controls, wage controls, heavy unionization, the conversion of factories to wartime production, the Depression-era faith in the problem-solving power of government, the conscription of a 16-million man army, and a top income tax rate of 94 percent.[83] To be sure, it was a different time with different challenges. America was built to defeat Nazism—and it did.

Tom Brokaw dubbed the generation that came of age during the Great Depression and subsequently won World War II, *the Greatest Generation.*

But he also gave it another name: *the GI Generation.*

Originally, the term GI referred to galvanized iron—a metal commonly used in the manufacture of US Army supplies and equipment. However, the initials soon came to mean *General Issue* or *Government Issue*, terms appropriate to the values of mass production and standardization that helped America win the war. It was the perfect name for a generation that came to view government as competent and effective.

Toward the end of the century, this Industrial model of government ran into trouble.

The first warning signs appeared in the 1970s, when Europe and Japan emerged from the wreckage of World War II and began to compete economically with the United States. Our economy started to globalize, a change that quickly accelerated when a handful of plucky engineers created the first personal computers in their garages. Today, the one-size-fits-all factory model of central planning still exists, but almost exclusively in the halls of government. Hell, even modern factories—built for greater consumer customization and rapidly evolving client needs—are, in some ways, less like old school factories than the federal government in Washington.

Obamacare is merely one product of this factory-style government. The feds are trying to fix modern healthcare problems with the same heavy-handed, standardized, top-down approach used to win World War II. However, wisely managing the care of millions is entirely different from deploying an army of millions—and the former is something for which government is wholly unsuited. It's like taking a sledgehammer to a fruit fly: They missed the fly and wrecked the living room, too. In a piece for Harvard's *Crimson*, Alex Castellanos smartly summed up the failure of the Industrial model succinctly, saying of the folks in Washington:

"This is not the worst they can do. This is this best they can do."[84]

Many Americans felt the same way in the 1930s, before FDR's revolution in government. They viewed Herbert Hoover's response to the Great Depression as woefully inadequate. What's remarkable is that Hoover was an exemplary manager, a celebrated humanitarian, widely considered one of the finest men of his time. Yet, his policies seemed out of step, relics of an antiquated agrarian model of government. When Franklin Roosevelt roared onto the scene, he proposed a slate of new government measures adhering to the Industrial model that had already changed the way Americans lived and worked. I do not think much of FDR's revolution. But I recognize that he was a man for his moment. While his policies leave much to be desired, his vision of government was consistent with the Industrial-scale challenges of his era.

Eighty years later, on the heels of George W. Bush's tumultuous presidency, it appeared to some that Barack Obama might be the next FDR; that he was custom-built for this moment in history. Now, he seems more like Herbert Hoover, minus the competence. Sure, Barack Obama's campaigns were modern. Yet, his presidency represents the last gasp of an old order. His administration has proven no more inventive, no less partisan, no more transparent, and no more forward thinking than any other in recent memory. On the contrary, from snooping on reporters to creating a governing climate conducive to IRS bullying to ramming through Obamacare to other troubling exercises of unilateral executive power, this administration has been much, much worse.

Sure, Millennials began their political lives with high hopes for Washington. That's changed. According to poll after poll, young Americans increasingly view the feds as wasteful and inefficient. Not surprisingly, they now favor market-oriented (read: *choice-based*) approaches to big problems, such as entitlement reform. After souring on Obamacare, they've grown deeply skeptical of heavy-handed, centralized solutions. Indeed, Millennials' frustration with government is starting to resemble a critique most commonly leveled by libertarians: government is too big to be honest.

It should come as no surprise that, regardless of who runs it, government is almost always the last to join the new era. In the 1930s, it was the last major mover in American life to adapt to the large-scale Industrial model that had already transformed economic and social life more than a generation earlier. This time around, government clings tightly to the outdated Industrial model of yesteryear: Standardized solutions, unionized workforces and production-line-style economic engineering.

Why? Well, consumers change quickly because they are self-interested—they *want* new products and services. Businesses change quickly because they are self-interested—they *want* new consumers. Even religions, if you'll pardon the blasphemy, change quickly because they are self-interested—they *want* new congregants. However, bureaucracies are not self-interested, per se, because they do not require self-interest to survive.

Participation in the marketplace or the religious space is purely optional, which makes businesses and churches sensitive to the wishes of their consumers and congregations. However, one cannot simply "opt-out" of funding the federal bureaucracy, which, ironically, shields it from the concerns of the very public it is intended to serve. Consequently, bureaucracy does not change until it is impossible for it to remain the same. That will happen once the first generation raised in the Information Age finally inherits the reigns of government power, bringing the "change" with them.

That's the Millennial, circa 2035.

When Millennials begin to rule the government roost in the 2030s, structural change *will* come. Not because Millennials are uniquely gifted or wise. Not because they are smarter or better than their parents. It will come because wherever Millennials go they bring the Information Age with them—they bring the ethos of choice with them, the sensibilities of an impatient, frugal, tech-snobby generation. They are, after all, unable to bring anything else. It is *who we are*, plain and simple.

This portends two significant changes for government: First, leaders will be forced to govern differently, and second, federal policymaking will begin to reflect greater personal choice.

Let's start with the politicians. Technology opens up new channels for dialogue and debate, not just on who deserves to win *Dancing with the Stars*, but on who deserves to lead. Speaking to *The New York Times'* Thomas Friedman, author Dov Seidman explains how this change alters the nature of political power:

'There are essentially just two kinds of authority: formal authority and moral authority [...] And moral authority is now so much more important than formal authority" in today's interconnected world, "where power is shifting to individuals who can easily connect and combine their power exponentially for good or ill."

You don't get moral authority just from being elected or born, said Seidman: "Moral authority is something you have to continue to earn by how you behave, by how you build trust with your people [...] Every time you exercise formal authority [...] you deplete it. Every time you exercise moral authority, leading by example, treating people with respect, you strengthen it."

Any leader who wants to lead just "by commanding power over people should think again," he added. "In this age, the only way to effectively lead is to generate power through people," said Seidman, because you have connected with them "in a way that earned their trust and enlisted them in a shared vision." [85]

When he first campaigned for president in 2008, Barack Obama effortlessly earned the trust of legions of Millennials. He commanded enormous *informal* influence. Upon becoming president, however, he quickly abused the *formal* power of his office: Obamacare, snooping on reporters, tolerating a lawless IRS, presiding over corruption at the VA, expanding the NSA's spying program, and flat-out refusing to enforce certain laws. These political missteps and scandals have eroded his informal authority and, with it, his ability to affect legislative change. Now, as the president once imperiously declared, he is left only with his pen and his phone.

So much for change.

Those in power—namely those who incline toward statism—will find their heavy-handed, one-sided approach to governing frustrated by a combination of 24-7 news coverage, social media, and alternative, user-generated journalism.[86] Only thoughtful leaders who seek to first exercise *informal* authority will have the support of the people, and by extension, the powerful. Only with *informal* authority can a leader build consensus for change.

The second change in government deals directly with federal policymaking and is best illustrated by example: In the 2030s, a 20 thousand page regulatory monstrosity like Obamacare will be almost inconceivable. For Millennials, technology isn't just a tool; it's something of an ethos. Sure, it's created some irritating social habits (texting at dinner), occasional narcissism (inane tweets about puerile subjects), and a touch of ADD. Nevertheless, it's also fostered strident individualism, an insistence on Steve Jobs-style simplicity, and a nearly fanatical intolerance of dysfunction.

The tech effect has made Millennials intensely impatient when it comes to the products and services they buy. Put simply, they expect things to work *as advertised*. It's not really surprising. In the early 80s, there was basically one phone company—AT&T. Today, competition and near-constant creative destruction has shaped the brand-averse Millennial; made him happy to discard yesterday's tech with the same enthusiasm with which he job-hops, church-shops, or bargain-hunts.

Massive regulatory behemoths are at odds, fundamentally, with the Information Age notions of simplicity, choice, and user-friendliness on which Millennials have been raised. Modern technology and its emphasis on personal choice not only decentralizes power, amplifies the influence of the individual, reduces the barriers for communication, idea-development, and enterprise; it changes the expectation of the user, the consumer, *the citizen*. It leads us to expect results, *quickly*. It leads us to expect transparency, dialogue and choice, *now*. We get mad when it doesn't work like that—which is one reason we're almost always mad at Washington these days.

Millennials' frugal nature and frustration with dysfunction will bode well for Washington. Does this mean every government office will be staffed with hoodie-sporting, flip-flop-wearing, Instagram-cruising, kick-off-the-day-at-ten-o'clock Millennials? No, but in the same way that corporations and churches now celebrate flexibility and choice, the future portends a smarter, slimmer government that does fewer things but does them better.

Millennials' choice-oriented reform instincts will bolster—and, in turn, be bolstered by—*two key structural developments*: First, the decline of unions; and second, the reform of the welfare state.

It will start with unions. They're already in decline, but by the mid-2030s they will become odd artifacts of a bygone era, confined mostly to government. Eventually, public employee unions' long war against their bosses—the taxpayers—will finally end with the disintegration of the unions themselves. Shortly thereafter, automation will alleviate pressure on the federal budget and smart politicians will finally be free to return power to state and—perhaps even more importantly—*local* governments, which are already far more credible due to their smaller size and, inherently, greater responsiveness.

With unions receding, Washington will be free to change how it operates. The Industrial model of government-as-service-provider will be replaced with an Information Age model of government-as-service-*procurer*. Expect *more* federal contractors and *fewer* federal employees as private sector companies and charitable organizations—both of which are preferred change-vehicles by Millennials— increasingly provide direct-to-citizen services.

At the same time, momentum to reform the welfare state will build. Pension-style Social Security will be altered to include some form of personal accounts, which Millennials (even, somewhat surprisingly, Millennial Democrats) overwhelmingly support. Single-payer Medicare will be overhauled to incorporate market-style (again, read: *choice-based*) competition among care providers— though government fiats coupled with individual mandates do not create a market (I'm looking at you, Obamacare). And here, once again, surveys indicate uncommonly broad support for Medicare reforms among Millennials, who support such programs but have grown distrustful of government's stewardship of them.

Entrepreneurial non-profits will continue their rise and aging welfare programs that trap struggling Americans in cycles of poverty will be exchanged, slowly, stubbornly and imperfectly, for new models that harness the entrepreneurial power of America's robust (and increasingly inventive) non-profit sector, deploying programs that put people to work, not to sleep.

These developments will strengthen *three* of the *Five Pillars of American Power—Economic Dynamism, Cultural Universality,* and *Domestic Stability*—which are predicated on the primacy of "The Individual" in American life. Right now, these pillars are buckling under the weight of the regulatory state, the nanny state, and the security state—last gasps of the old order. However, by the mid-

2030s Millennials will finally bring to government what Boomers began in their garages: The tech effect. This choice-focused ethos will strengthen *Economic Dynamism, Cultural Universality* and *Domestic Stability*, as follows:

America's *Economic Dynamism* depends upon the pioneering instincts of our nation's entrepreneurs, scientists, and explorers. It relies upon the initiative and creativity of American workers, the sacred stature of the trailblazer and the risk-taker. Demographers have found that Millennials revere the entrepreneur and consider small business ownership the ideal vehicle for their aspirations, unlike prior generations, which preferred the social movement or the political campaign. It makes sense. We were raised in an era of intrepid tech titans—improbable entrepreneurs who reshaped the world with disruptive technologies. They didn't tear down the system; they remade it—bettered it. And while government faltered and failed, fumbling from one nail-biting crisis to another, these upstarts changed the world. An increasingly choice-based model of government will reflect the special status of the American entrepreneur, strengthening *Economic Dynamism*.

America's *Cultural Universality* stems from our obsession with personal choice. Whether it's building a playlist, customizing a car, choosing a career, or buying jeans and Coca-Cola, the American brand is based on the endless options and opportunities afforded to the individual. A government that acts in accord with these values domestically will be able to make a more credible case for American values abroad—carving out a foreign policy path somewhere in between President Bush's aggressive, transformational unilateralism and President Obama's craven, destabilizing approach.

America's *Domestic Stability* is linked to healthy civic institutions and our respect for the Rule of Law, both of which are organized around the freedom of the individual, not the state. Hence, we are presumed innocent until proven guilty, afforded due process, guaranteed equal access to justice, and protected from the whims of the majority. By the late 2030s, America's public institutions will be smaller; its private social institutions, bigger. More power will be devolved to state and local governments, reflecting Millennials' cultural instincts, which have already boosted "buy local" movements across the country. Ironically, global connectivity will promote the localization of power. Only when institutions are smaller will they be positioned to regain lost credibility.

Right now, on the cusp of this *Great Transition*, things feel a lot like adolescence. It's hard. It's awkward. You think you know what you're doing, but you don't, because you've never done it before.

You want to cling to the past and race to the future all at once. Periods of intense optimism and intense pessimism are punctuated by moments of intense embarrassment. Nothing quite fits. You may even want to go backward. That's what most of our politicians want—to return to the comfortable days of a bygone era, when geopolitics made sense, people were relatively easy to appease, and a government based on the Industrial model worked reasonably well. Big bureaucracies. Top-down programs. Sledgehammer solutions. But they only want to go back because they can't imagine what a new model for government looks like. Forget about them. The Information Age—*adulthood*—awaits us.

And it's the age of "Big Individual" not "Big Government."

Today, people can build communities online, conduct commerce online, renew relationships online, share ideas online, advocate, teach, learn, debate, and donate online—anywhere, anytime, with anyone from nearly any device. The modern community space—catalyzed by technology—is vast, vibrant, and dynamic *without* government. It has organized itself spontaneously, according to countless *individual* preferences in a happy, natural arrangement.

What central planner could have organized us thusly? We do not need government to convene us. We have convened ourselves. We do not need government to decide for us. We can decide for ourselves. We do not need government to bring us together. We are already together.

This is not the case against community. On the contrary, this is the case against coercion. We have already constructed the communities of the new century—we don't need Washington in the middle. In the coming age, the federal government must learn to engage the power of private social institutions and win the support of the people by applying *informal* authority. It must learn to return power to smaller governments, or the people. If it does not, its institutions will continue to crumble.

Of course, Washington's *Great Transition* from Industrial to Information Age will be fraught with political turmoil and, potentially, social unrest as government's various client groups fight over ever-shrinking shares of the Washington pie. Reforming the entitlement system, in particular, is likely to involve biblical-scale wailing and gnashing of the teeth. However, as author and practical conservative Herbert Stein once noted, "if something cannot go on forever, it will stop."[87] In other words, if the entitlement system is not reformed—if government is not reformed—it will collide headlong with the practical cruelties of mathematics. Since government *cannot* grow indefinitely, it *will not* grow indefinitely.

Hopefully, government will undergo the *Great Transition* with a modicum of wisdom, in full recognition of the fact that it has no practical alternative. However, if it does not conform to the needs of our time, it will, ultimately and painfully, succumb to the forces of mathematics. In the end, math always wins.

And no matter what, we will finally have our long-awaited change.

CHAPTER 6
THE THRILL IS GONE

"Every presidency falls short of the expectations that the candidate sets. But no man has ever promised more and delivered less than the current occupant of the Oval Office."[88]
- Peter Wehner

Millennials elected Barack Obama. Many now regret it.

But back in the heady days of late 2012, liberal pundits indulged in a happy fiction. Barack Obama had launched a new age of liberalism, they imagined. Faith in government had been strengthened, they said. Millennials are destined to become permanent wards of a rising Democrat Party, they fully believed.

This fantasy is now unraveling. Why?

Let's go back to 2008.

Millennials' newly minted president was swept into office amidst economic upheaval and historically high expectations. "Yes, we can!" was a new slogan for a new generation, mindlessly chanted by hordes of zombielike groupies at jam-packed rallies across the country. But promises of economic revitalization, transparent government, and forward-looking policymaking never came to fruition. Instead, we got Obamacare, bailouts, a pork-laden stimulus package, and cheap platitudes from our new president such as, "I never said change would be easy."

"Well, he can't run on *change* twice," I told a colleague in the summer of 2009.

And he didn't. In 2012, President Obama—vicar of hope and change—jettisoned the feel-good mantra of 2008 in favor of a much harsher, bare-knuckled approach. Ironically, he would run a reelection campaign strikingly similar to that of the man he so often castigated as arrogant, out-of-touch, and altogether un-changey: George W. Bush.

Like President Bush, Obama faced sagging poll numbers in the months before Election Day—sometimes barely above and sometimes just below the all-important 50 percent mark. Like Bush, Obama focused on turning out his base instead of tacking to the middle. Like Bush, Obama moved quickly to reshape the race around the personal qualities of his opponent.

So long hope and change; we hardly knew ye.

Barack Obama's reelection campaign was premised neither on change nor his dubious slate of first-term accomplishments. Instead, he campaigned on the foibles of his opponent. Mitt Romney, Obama suggested, was a heartless plutocrat who couldn't possibly understand, let alone sympathize with the plight of ordinary Americans. To the amazement (and dejection) of conservatives, strange side issues began to creep into the presidential contest. How many cars did Mitt Romney have? Was he a bully in high school? Did he really strap his dog to the roof of his car and travel cross-country?

Obama, if he could not fix your problems, pretended to understand them. This vacuous platform returned the president to the White House with, if it is possible, an agenda even thinner than "hope and change."

As a result, he was the first president in the modern era to win reelection with *fewer* votes than he garnered the first time around.[89] And while some on the Left have grown fond of comparing him to Ronald Reagan, the comparisons don't hold up under scrutiny. Barack Obama beat Mitt Romney by 4 percent in 2012, less than his 7-point victory over John McCain in 2008. On the other hand, Reagan won reelection in a genuine landslide—winning 49 states, trouncing Walter Mondale by 18 points, and besting his own 1980 victory by 8 points.[90]

In fact, Barack Obama's reelection victory is uninspiring by almost any measure. He won 51 percent of the vote in 2012, compared to 60 percent for FDR in 1936, 57 percent for Eisenhower in 1956, and 58 percent for Reagan in 1984.[91] And now, Obama's presidency—once imagined to be transformational—has become nothing short of an historic letdown. There are practical consequences for a president who seeks reelection primarily on the basis of his opponent's shortcomings rather than his own first-term record. It usually spells trouble for his second term.

Consider the all-important *mandate*.

Once elected, nearly every president claims to have won a

mandate—backing from the American people to pursue the agenda on which he ran. The success with which a president pursues that mandate is a key measure of his effectiveness. However, Barack Obama has no practical policy mandate whatsoever. This isn't due to the margin of his victory but rather the emptiness of his platform.

The president's signature legislative achievements—the Stimulus and the Affordable Care Act—were political liabilities of the highest order. He did not run *on* them. He ran *from* them. Indeed, he campaigned on very little, other than class warfare rhetoric aimed at his opponent.

In that respect, the president's only real second-term mandate is to be someone other than Mitt Romney. Not very inspiring, but it helps explain the constant drivel from the White House about income inequality in lieu of practical proposals for private sector job creation, which would, of course, promote greater social mobility.

So, where does that leave us? Welcome back to 2014.

For Millennials, the thrill is gone. In the immediate aftermath of the Obamacare train wreck, the president's approval rating among young voters slipped below 40 percent. Fewer than half of Millennials say they would reelect him. A majority of voters under 25 even want to recall him from office.[92]

I think the official word for that is impeachment.

Millennial support for the president first slipped below 50 percent in the wake of the NSA snooping and IRS creeping scandals. Little more than a month after the Obamacare rollout, a mere 36 percent of 18 to 29 year-olds said they approved of the president's job performance—3 points lower than the national average reported in the same poll.[93]

Late-wave Millennials just now entering their early voting years are being shaped by the politics of Obamacare and attendant scandals, such as the Veterans Affairs healthcare tragedies. Less than two months after suffering a humiliating defeat in the government shutdown fight, Republicans became the beneficiaries of Democrats' Obamacare self-destruction.[94]

Among 18 to 29 year olds, the much-hated Republicans in Congress suddenly gained a 10-point advantage on the economy, a 5-point advantage on healthcare, and a 3-point advantage on the budget. In fact, on matters of healthcare and the economy, young voters gave Republicans larger advantages than did the general voting population.[95]

That's quite a turnabout.

From the time immediately following President Obama's second inauguration to the period immediately after the Obamacare rollout, voters under 30 abandoned the president they twice elected in staggering numbers. Barack Obama's support among Millennials fell by 23 points—worse than any other group. In the month following the Obamacare rollout, overall opposition to the new law rose by 16 points among young voters. Strong opposition increased by 21 points.[96]

It's not just Obamacare.

By the end of 2013, support for the president's agenda had collapsed. Fewer than 40 percent of *Millennials* approved of his handling of healthcare, the economy, and Iran. Fewer than 30 percent said he was doing a good job managing the budget deficit. Disapproval also extended to the president's once-ironclad personal ratings, including trustworthiness. By 2014, a nonstop stream of scandals—from corruption at the VA to the mess at the border to a series of foreign policy fumbles—kept the president under water on Millennials' top issues.[97] [98]

The president's job approval rating may stabilize or it may continue to sink. Regardless, with his support on key issues deeply eroded, Barack Obama's ability to affect lasting change has been permanently compromised. He cannot turn Obamacare into a net positive, erase it from the memories of impressionable young voters, or forever delay the second wave of policy cancellations it is sure to trigger, unless he simultaneously dismantles the very law that colloquially bears his name. Barack Obama's failures have not only tarnished his legacy, they've shattered faith in government and left liberalism in ruins. Six years ago, Barack Obama's candidacy made Millennials receptive to the argument that government is transcendent, argues Harvard pollster John Della Volpe. [99]   To become a truly transformative president, Barack Obama had only to prove that his solutions were, in fact, *solutions.*

Of course, he *could* not—because they *were* not.

Barack Obama not only failed to overcome Washington's gridlock, he became the very source of it. To the extent that he is the victim of circumstances, they are circumstances he created. Rather than addressing the economic crisis that left millions jobless, Barack Obama led a tin-eared campaign for a monstrous healthcare bill, which passed without a single Republican vote. This devoutly partisan legislation—and the troubling tactics used to pass it— created the Tea Party and forever soured relations with the GOP.

Barack Obama made it clear: For him to win, Republicans had to lose.

This was a far cry from the unifying, post-partisan promises of Candidate Obama. But for Democrats, it was more than a broken promise—it was a missed opportunity. Barack Obama's historic victory in 2008 might have become an FDR moment that validated Millennials' faith in big government and inaugurated a second "New Deal." But his policies flopped. Instead of celebrating government, young Americans have grown more distrustful of it.

In some cases, *deepy* distrustful.

In 2008, 69 percent of Millennials said, "government should do more to solve big problems." [100] Today, only 34 percent say it should "take an active role," while 61 percent disagree. 2-to-1, Millennials say the federal government is hurting, rather than helping the economy. Nearly 3-to-1, young Americans say the federal government should cut taxes, while only 11 percent are for more federal spending and a mere 16 percent think the federal government should be bigger.[101]

Nearly 3-to-1, young Americans say, "politics today is no longer able to meet the challenges our country is facing." Compared to prior generations, Millennials are less interested in government career tracks, with just 6 percent of college students saying they want to work in the public sector. That's because Millennials strongly desire meaningful employment and they no longer consider government work meaningful. Liberals bemoan this trend. Conservatives should celebrate it. We don't need more federal workers—we need more entrepreneurs. [102]

Even prior to the Obamacare rollout, 51 percent of Millennials said that government-run programs tend to be wasteful and inefficient—up from 31 percent in 2003. They now decisively support free trade and decisively oppose Affirmative Action. A whopping 74 percent of Millennials believe Medicare should carry private insurance, with an astounding 86 percent backing some form of Social Security privatization—including 51 percent of young *Democrats.*[103]

In many respects, this is *not* the same generation that elected Obama in 2008.

Partly, it's because Barack Obama has pissed off his own voters. And partly, it's because new Millennials—those just now joining the electorate—are less likely to call themselves liberals, Democrats, or Obama supporters than their slightly older Millennial peers. In fact, 42 percent of *younger* Millennials identify as conservatives, roughly the same as the general population. That compares with only a third of older Millennials. And while older Millennials are roughly 20-points more likely to identify as Democrat than Republican, younger 18-to-19 year-olds are only 3-points more likely to consider themselves Democrat than Republican, making them, somewhat surprisingly, slightly *more Republican* than the general population.[104] [105]

Some analysts ascribe the increased conservatism among younger Millennials to the weak job market. [106] That's probably true, but it's only part of the explanation.

Older Millennials still remember the War in Iraq, the Patriot Act, and the market crash of 2008—major events that largely animated their opposition to George W. Bush and their support of Barack Obama. Those events had far less political impact on late-wave Millennials. Instead, Millennials under 25 are coming of age during the failed presidency of Barack Obama.[107]

And they vote like it.

When Republican Ken Cuccinelli lost his 2013 bid for Governor of Virginia, exit polls showed that he lost 25 to 29 year-olds (older Millennials) by 15 points. However, despite losing the election by nearly 3 points, Cuccinelli actually *won* 18 to 24-year-olds (younger Millennials) by a comfortable 6-point margin—45 percent to 39 percent. And that's in spite of a stronger-than-usual Libertarian candidate, who most observers say siphoned votes away from Cuccinelli.[108]

Statistical coincidence? It's doesn't seem like it. In his recall election, Wisconsin Governor Scott Walker won 18 to 24 year-olds, too. And in New Jersey, Chris Christie improved on his 2009 performance among 18 to 29 year-olds by 10 points.

What is most interesting (and perhaps illustrative) about Christie's win is that, despite capturing 60 percent of the vote in 2013 (compared to his 52 percent share in 2009), his performance among 30 to 44 year-olds remained flat. Let me repeat that: Christie picked up 8-points overall, 10-points among 18 to 29 year-olds, but *did not* improve on his 2009 performance among 30 to 44 year-olds.

Why?

It's likely that Christie's outsized gains among 18 to 29 year-olds are owed, at least in part, to younger Millennials—18 to 24 year-olds—joining the voting rolls for the first time. While his lack of gains among 30 to 44 year-olds is due, at least in part, to older, more liberal Millennials entering their thirties.[109]

Regardless of the reasons, the Christie win in New Jersey disproves the arrogant notion that demographics are destiny; that whole generations can *belong* to certain political parties. Chris Christie tackled the Teacher's Union, supported traditional marriage, cut spending, lowered taxes, slashed Planned Parenthood, *and* won the Hispanic vote, won Independent women, and won self-identified moderates—all in a deep blue state.

As much damage as Barack Obama did to his party, Democrats may have an even tougher time winning big races without him.

Obama's candidacy created conditions uniquely favorable to the Left—conditions unlikely to be present in future cycles. For example, it's unlikely that Democrats can depend on the record-high African American turnout that typified the Obama years and exceeded that of whites (for the first time) in 2012.[110]

Despite twin wins in 2008 and 2012, Obama's presidency has left Democrats structurally weaker than when he first took office. They've "lost nine governorships, 56 members of the House, and two Senate seats," notes former Clinton advisor Doug Sosnik. But it's worse than that. Barack Obama's 2010 shellacking left Republicans with 680 new state legislative seats and positioned the GOP well for redistricting. [111]

Sosnik titled his memo on post-Obama politics, "America ... Still Looking for Change that it Can Believe In."

That about sums it up.

Barack Obama was a generational *candidate*—but not a transformational president. His time in the White House will leave the country bitterly divided. In the aftermath of Obamacare, the same fate may befall the Democrat party. He will leave his party immensely weaker than when he found it. His presidency has proven government anemic, rather than muscular—incompetent, rather than thoughtful. His policy failures have proven the lie of liberalism and saved the GOP from its own self-destructive impulses.

That sets up the GOP's real challenge for the coming decade. Republicans won't win elections simply by inflicting less damage to their brand than Democrats—the Left has too great a structural advantage at this point. Instead, the conservative movement must emphasize commonalities between a timeless conservative philosophy based on individual rights and Millennials' emerging culture, which is based on personal choice.

The connections are clear.

First, it's time to become the smart party; the party of heroic entrepreneurs not crony capitalists. Millennials revere entrepreneurship and many, regardless of whether or not they actually own a small business, describe their attitude toward life as entrepreneurial.

Second, Millennials have adopted a somewhat laissez-faire outlook on many public policy matters and consider certain GOP social positions inconsistent with the oft-stated conservative belief in personal liberty. The best word to describe the Millennial viewpoint on social matters is libertarian. This critique has merit and liberty-loving conservatives should not casually dismiss it. Instead, we should seek to emphasize the choice-driven elements of our conservative philosophy.

Thirdly, we must field candidates who brim with optimism. Ronald Reagan inspired voters, particularly young voters, by telling them they did not have to settle for lesser lives; that America was a place built for risk-taking and dream-chasing; that individuals can be big, only when government is small. His optimism stood in stark contrast to Jimmy Carter's whimpering pessimism. In this case, past is prelude. Of all generations, Millennials remain the most optimistic about the future, despite grim conditions. They are looking for a party that shares this outlook, a candidate who believes they've got a shot. In darkening economic times, they signed on to *Candidate* Obama's message of hope. But *President* Obama proved government could not get the job done. The GOP's next nominee will have to remind Americans that just because government can't do it, doesn't mean it can't be done.

In the past two presidential elections, Democrats have found a way to capitalize on the Millennial's laissez-faire, live-and-let-live attitudes on social matters. They've persuaded young voters that same sex marriage is the civil rights issue of our day. They have convinced Millennials to vote for the party of slower growth, fewer jobs, and bigger debt by taking the focus *off* economics and shifting it *on* to social policy. They've guided young voters to select the liberal label on the basis of their social libertarianism. Eventually, Republicans will learn to embrace their inner economic populists. At the same time, as more Millennials fill the party's voting rolls, we'll start seeing viable GOP candidates emerge on the other side of the same sex marriage issue. If such issues recede from the spotlight or become a wash in national debates, the GOP will have an easier time bypassing Millennials' knee-jerk social liberalism and, for the first time, converting their finely tuned (and politically untapped) fiscal instincts into concrete votes.

Economic freedom is not a political liability. It is our sole political strength.

Unless controversial issues like immigration split the party and hand Democrats the internecine GOP war they want, the GOP stands a better chance with Hispanic voters, too. After all, "younger Hispanics feel less of an allegiance to the Democratic Party than their elders," writes Sosnik. Fully 59 percent of Hispanics over 55 identify as Democrats. Among Millennial Hispanics, that number slides to 50 percent. Similarly, while 50 percent of Asian voters—the second-faster growing group in America—consider themselves Democrats,

73 percent voted for Barack Obama. Democrats cannot expect this level of minority conversion in future elections, without Obama's generational candidacy in the mix. A charismatic Republican who masters the right tone and tenor could easily make in-roads with both Asian and Hispanic voters.[112]

It's hard for politicians, pundits, and even voters marinated in the old politics to imagine a *new* politics. But the new voter is different—really different. She's less ideological, less label conscious. In fact, she may not even recognize the labels that dominated yesteryear's political lexicon. She instinctively favors small and not big. She may very well consider herself a fiscal conservative. She thinks the national debt, and perhaps by extension, China, is a big problem. However, she's repulsed by the GOP's views on same sex marriage. She voted *for* Barack Obama in 2008 but *against* Mitt Romney in 2012.

She's still waiting for *change she can believe in.*

For the last five years, conservatives have, understandably, fixated on Barack Obama. His policies will leave our nation undeniably worse off; deeper in debt, plagued by lackluster growth and entrenched in the very Washington gridlock he pledged to overcome. Conservatives are aggravated by Obama's constant campaigning—for every problem, every crisis, the president's sole solution seems to be *more campaigning.* In every debt-ceiling debate or budget showdown, the president tries to play the detached victim, hovering transcendently above debate, not really a participant, never taking responsibility for the outcome. He lambastes the dysfunction in Washington as if he had no part in creating it. He practices the most cynical, partisan politics of any modern president; abuses the power of the office more than any president since Nixon; presides over one of the most closed, opaque, insulated White Houses in history—all while wearing the mask of a reasonable man, a man of compromise, transparency, and thoughtfulness. This galls conservatives.

But we need to let him go.

Forget him. Like a magician whose tricks are spent, Barack Obama has lost his hypnotic hold on the public. When he campaigned, he campaigned like no other. But his campaigns are over. No one is listening anymore. His administration is beset upon by scandal and incompetence. His legislative accomplishments are limited to a failed Stimulus and an unpopular healthcare law so dysfunctional that it has been routinely delayed and dismantled by the very people who devised it. Barack Obama's presidency—piled high with empty promises and broken dreams—will be remembered

mostly for its *unmet expectations.*
     It's time to imagine a post-Obama politics.

CHAPTER 7
DON'T LABEL ME, BRO

Millennials are fickle.

A bunch of job-hopping, bargain-shopping, label-dropping miscreants ... the whole lot of 'em. And yet, Millennials' pathological resistance to branding is something of a silver lining for conservatives. This label-averse generation is as disloyal to political parties as it is to retailers, restaurants, phone companies, and all the rest.

That may explain why, though they lean Democrat, they continue to express little devotion to the party they twice empowered. Notably, the Obama years have not produced a surge in Democrat party registration. On the contrary, we've seen the percentage of *independents* skyrocket—among Millennials in particular. Today, fully *half* of this generation's voters consider themselves political independents. [113] [114] Yes, most presently tilt left, particularly on social issues. But calling yourself an Independent is political short-hand for, "I'm a free agent."

Isn't it also short for, "I'm uninformed?"

Often, yes. However, "Independent" isn't the same as "Third Party." We're not talking about a cohesive or monolithic bloc of voters. Sure, some Independents are politically unaligned simply because they're politically unaware. Others are genuine moderates. A few are too extreme for either major party. Most, however, have distinct political leanings—Republican or Democrat—but *still* refuse to pick a party.

Those of us who eat, sleep, and drink nitty-gritty public policy tend to overestimate its importance in presidential contests. Yet, many general election voters are neither label conscious nor intensely principled. Indeed, national elections are certainly *influenced* but seldom *decided* solely on the basis of a candidate's positions because, after all, voters are not machines that objectively analyze candidate platforms and cast their ballots accordingly. If they were, Mitt Romney would be president.

Today, the decision to register "Independent" is not necessarily a sign of political ignorance or indecisiveness. Increasingly, it's something of a protest vote. And in this protest-vote climate, it's not just party brands that are losing prominence. Gradually, some of my favorite time-honored political buzzwords are losing their power, too. There is one politically-charged term, in particular, that almost every American voter instinctively understands—*except* Millennials.

Big Government.

For conservatives, these words are charged with political power. After all, almost everyone remembers that famous line from Ronald Reagan's first inaugural: "Government is not the solution to our problems; government *is* the problem." Almost everyone remembers Bill Clinton's famous State of the Union pronouncement that "the era of big government is over."

That is, almost everyone except Millennials.

Most of us are too young. Our political memory is largely limited to George W. Bush and Barack Obama—two back-to-back big government presidencies during which the issue of government's size seldom drove the national debate. I know it's hard to imagine that a term as politically-charged as "big government" could hold much less meaning for Millennials, but as far as we can recall, government has always been big. The debt has always been big. Washington has always been big.

Ask a Millennial what he thinks about big government and ask for sweet tea in the Deep South. You'll get the same answer: Is there any other kind?

That's why Millennials' support for big government was never ideological—they did not favor big government solutions per se; they simply did not fear them or regard them as inherently worse than private sector solutions. Sure, Millennials distrust *big* everything—from government to business. However, the term *big government* is not chockfull of the same derogatory, political significance that it carries for other age groups. Studies suggest that traditional political hierarchies, such as big government vs. small government, and dualities, such as Republican vs. Democrat, are less important to Millennials than to prior generations. [115]

Conservatives face *two challenges* when talking to this label-averse generation:

First, for several decades, liberals have had nearly total power over the public school, the college classroom, the newsroom, the TV set, and the movie theater. This nearly uncontested control over America's *Cultural Drivers* has yielded enormous dividends for the Left, in the form of knee-jerk liberalism among under-informed young voters, particularly on social issues. While this is a largely undefined, superficial species of liberalism driven by the momentary influences of ill-considered campus communism or left-leaning TV programming, it's certainly present and, right now, it's the Millennial's operating political default—much like the factory settings on your TV. Smart conservative candidates must learn to carefully navigate these liberal defaults—particularly those that deal with thorny social issues or matters of economic equality—before attempting to change them.

Second, Millennials came of age in a very flat and informal post-Cold War world, free of the hierarchies and rigid ideologies that dominated the politics of previous generations. They weren't afraid of the Hun or the Red Menace. And they neither invented nor widened nor narrowed the social safety net. They didn't live through FDR or LBJ and they don't really remember Ronald Reagan. The War on Terrorism, which might have defined them in traditional, symmetrical terms, quickly became a political football and has since been all but abandoned by the Obama administration.

Politically, Millennials don't really color within the lines.

Driven by an overriding choice-ethos, quite a few Millennials favor robust economic freedom and robust social liberty, too. We'd call that a libertarian streak. At the same time, this generation's greater racial diversity has also given rise to the reverse pairing—economic liberalism and social conservatism.

That means *personal* brands are essential.

With traditional information shortcuts (big government, for example) in decline and self-identified Independents on the rise, the new politics will be increasingly personality-driven. Keep it mind that Millennials haven't yet benefited from a conservative icon, like Ronald Reagan, who articulated sensible, small government values and used persuasive, powerful rhetoric to package his ideas. As a result, their political *principles* are frequently insubstantial, particularly on economic matters.

Unfortunately for traditional GOP candidates, Millennials' most intense opinions tend to be on the social issues with which they have greater experience, such as same-sex marriage. They are unlikely to grow out of these opinions, which were formed from genuine, real-world experiences. On the other hand, their negative experience with economic liberalism offers hope to conservatives, who can fashion economic messages aimed at arousing this generation's instinctive frugality and entrepreneurialism.

When speaking to younger crowds, expect successful GOP candidates to emphasize economic issues, to speak optimistically, and to cultivate a comfortable, authentic personal image, while devoutly avoiding the forced sound-biting of forgotten buzzwords. GOP candidates must reexamine their rhetoric—reconsider how they describe problems and solutions—if they're going to appeal to young voters who are not fluent in the vernacular of prior generations and who, as a rule, are reasonably brand-averse. They must speak a new political language.[116]

That was easy for liberals.

After all, they spent several generations polluting the word *liberal* before dumping it in favor of another word: *Progressive.*

Plucked from Europe's *Age of Enlightenment,* the term *progressive* is, traditionally speaking, ideologically distinct from modern liberalism. Once upon a time, progressivism referred to the broadly Western idea that science, technology, reason, and economics can, when properly harnessed, improve society. The old school, European progressive believed in applying scientific principles to government—thinking that these principles, which prize empirical analysis above knee-jerk impulse, are sound predicates for good statecraft.

Progressivism in the United States was somewhat different. A product of rapid, large-scale industrialization, American progressivism emerged in the late 19th Century as an alternative to the classical liberalism of America's Founders. Indeed, progressives expressly rejected the revolutionary principles of 1776, repudiated the idea of sovereign individualism, and abhorred the notion of expansive, natural rights. President Woodrow Wilson was their champion:

"We are not bound to adhere to the doctrines held by the signers of the Declaration of Independence: we are as free as they were to make and unmake governments. We are not here to worship men or a document. [...] Every Fourth of July should be a time for examining our standards, our purposes, for determining afresh what principles, what forms of power we think most likely to effect our safety and happiness. That and that alone is the obligation the Declaration lays upon us."[117]

If you've ever heard of the idea of a "living, breathing constitution," this is where it comes from. Progressives favored a new concept of rights and freedom, based on a powerful, active state. To accomplish such a transformation, they needed to reimagine the individual's relationship with government and redefine the very nature of freedom.   Suddenly, government was no longer in the business of simply *protecting* rights—it was in the business of *creating* them. A government that can create rights assumes power over those rights.

It's important to note that early American progressives were *not* socially liberal. They typically supported traditional values and used the state to enforce them—a significant difference from today's strident, socially liberal progressives.

Turn-of-the-century progressivism has been dead for decades—which made it perfectly suitable for a leftwing revival. Of course, this "rebranding" is superficial. Whether he calls himself a liberal or a progressive, he cares little for the historical distinctions and seeks boldly, plainly to empower the state, not the individual. Whatever justification liberal spinmeisters may conjure up for the sudden resurgence of the term, it seems plain that the Left has merely appropriated the progressive label now that liberalism is thoroughly worn out.

That type of brand swapping was easy for liberals.   Not conservatives.

For better or worse, the conservative has had a lot more trouble finding the right words to describe herself, let alone talk to Millennials. She sticks to her words, even when they're poor fits. Just look at the term *conservative* itself. It's not a very good description of the modern liberty movement, for *two reasons*:

First, American conservatives are not scions of the tree of European conservatism. That is, they were never Monarchists; they are not proponents of state power. Today's pro-liberty conservative is really descended from *classical liberalism.* She believes the individual, not the state, is sovereign. The classical liberal believes that her rights, as described in the Declaration of Independence, are unalienable, meaning that they cannot be given or taken away. Her rights are *natural*—they belong to her and her alone. And unlike the Progressive's expansive state, the conservative's limited government is powerless to create rights—but equally powerless to eliminate them.

However, in certain social matters the American conservative actually looks more like a *19th Century progressive* than a *classical liberal.* For example, the conservative's defense of traditional marriage aims to protect existing social structures and privileges—to concentrate power rather than diffuse it. In this way, many social conservatives actually resemble early American progressives.

Secondly, with the welfare state now firmly ensconced, today's true conservative is more scrappy underdog than guardian of the status quo. He seeks to reform Social Security, Medicare, and Medicaid; to overhaul the tax structure and reduce the welfare state; to reign in the regulatory regime and eliminate state-sponsored subsidies. He wishes to do away with protectionism, mercantilism, and crony capitalism—to change the status quo and enact policies that favor expansive individualism. Today's conservative is less a conservative and more a reformer.

Words matter. How we describe ourselves matters. Ultimately, it affects how voters think of us. And right now, the GOP is viewed neither as the party of liberty nor the party of choice. And absent the power of its small government label, it stands only for big business and intolerance in the mind of younger voters.

Basically, our words—our brand—suck.

Of course, this won't change if conservatives simply acquiesce, under duress, to immigration reform. It will not change if the Republican Party commissions a brilliant study (as much as I love reading them) and realigns the language of its platform. It will not change if GOP candidates, in a fit of political opportunism, suddenly jettison their long-standing social values overnight. And certainly, contrary to the advice of liberals, the GOP cannot fix its brand simply by becoming more liberal (but thanks for the advice, guys).

However, over the next two decades, *three key developments* will converge to bring about *authentic* change. Together, these developments will rehabilitate the Republican brand: First, a change at the top of the ticket; second, a change in the politics of Millennials; and third, a change in the composition of the GOP.

First, *a change at the top of the ticket*: Republicans will finally field a presidential candidate who can speak to Millennials. Democrats wandered in the wilderness for nearly fifty years in between the charismatic candidacies of John Kennedy and Barack Obama. Our candidate may already be in the field, contemplating a run in 2016. It's also possible we'll need to wait until 2020 or 2024. But, inevitably, a generational candidate will emerge.

This candidate will not be Ronald Reagan.

However, like Reagan, he (or she) will master the art of optimism. He will intuitively recognize, as Reagan did, that fear does not pave the path to the White House. In the age of Barack Obama, conservatives have understandably spent most of their time talking about what government cannot do. However, we've spent precious little time talking about what individuals *can do.*

That's going to change. American conservatism is all about the heroic individual. It's not about settling for less or accepting a smaller life. It's about building a world without boundaries. At its best, authentic conservatism celebrates the beauty of personal choice, free from coercion; it honors entrepreneurship and creative destruction, rather than entrenched, generational economic hierarchy. The GOP's next big candidate will masterfully present these timeless conservative principles in contemporary textures and speak in a language that evokes the values of choice, thrift, and liberty.

The key is *authenticity*—a sacred tenet of the Church of the Millennial.

To many Millennials, the Republican Party's latest efforts to appeal to constituencies it previously ignored—against the backdrop of rancorous internal debate—lack authenticity. Say what you will of Millennials, and many criticisms are fair, but their antennae tend to go up when they detect blatant fakery.

The clever GOP candidate will master the effortless authenticity Barack Obama mustered for his 2008 run. On popular culture, Obama was fluent and unrehearsed. He was also self-aware. He recognized that he was 20 years older than his biggest fans and never appeared to pander; the music he listened to was age-appropriate, but good. His carefully cultivated celebrity was never overeager or ridiculous. His fashion was smart, but never a caricature.

On policy, the smart Republican candidate will campaign vigorously for choice-based reforms to the social safety net, the bureaucracy, and the regulatory state—entirely reimagining the outdated, Industrial-era system that has dominated Washington since FDR. She'll speak past her opponents, not to them, rebutting criticisms by describing detractors as old and out of touch. We're looking forward, not backward, she will say. Her reforms, however complex, will always be described in terms of the individual, the personal. She'll speak in narratives and be unafraid to use her personal story to make a point. She will use hope more often than fear.

Since the term *big government* fails to resonate with Millennials, the smart conservative candidate will instead exalt the individual—and accomplish the same goal. She won't shy away from talking about poverty, because she can confidently declare that free enterprise has rescued *billions* from destitution and hopelessness. She'll sing sonnets to the virtue of entrepreneurship and innovation, which will appeal to Millennials' deeply embedded cultural traits. She'll gore some sacred cows and blast a tax code that disadvantages the Middle Class; take a hatchet to corporate subsidies with as much fervor as government waste. In this way, the GOP's opposition to a bloated regulatory regime will be more credible, because it will be perceived as a service to liberty, not to lobbyists.

Second, *a change in the politics of Millennials*: The inevitable rise of a new Republican standard-bearer is likely to coincide with something of a shift among Millennials, too. As I'll explain in the *Turning Point*, generations *do not* simply grow more conservative with age. However, experience clearly creates conditions that help innate conservative traits surface. Paying taxes, supporting a family, making the mortgage, and running a business all encourage a generation's underlying conservative traits to factor more prominently into voting decisions. New experiences begin to interact with deeply embedded cultural features—such as religiosity, frugality, and openness, to name a few—creating new political cues. Real-world experience will lift up deep-seated cultural instincts: Economic conservatism will rise.

To be sure, Millennials will not transform into traditional conservatives. However, galvanized by candidates who finally speak their language, many will evolve into fiscally focused, reform-minded conservatives with finely tuned instincts for personal choice, on both social and economic matters.

This political evolution has been years in the making. Here's how it started:

Obama's candidacy awakened the left-leaning aspects of the Millennial's culture—namely social liberalism. Obama spoke to the souls of young, malleable voters, causing the Millennial's cultural instincts for tolerance, equality, and globalism to rise to the surface. Politically speaking, Obama is the equivalent of a first crush. And Millennials swooned. His appeals truly *did* speak to embedded cultural traits—in the same way that Kennedy spoke to Silents and Reagan spoke to Boomers. Obama's great talent was an ability to address the Millennials' liberal cultural impulses and turn them into political cues.

It worked something like this: *You, young Millennial, believe in community service because you like to help people. Since you like to help people, you should support a more active federal government, too. After all, we do good stuff.*

Right away, an experienced conservative would reject this idea because she understands that community service is best practiced at the local level, by private charities, churches, and individuals. An experienced conservative is also uncomfortable with an active federal government because he has *learned* to distrust it—and he knows that big government is expensive, wasteful and disruptive. Unless they are students of politics, young voters lack a frame of reference for true conservative governance and simply associated conservatism with the social and national security policies of the Bush administration.

In the days leading up to his inauguration, Barack Obama was hailed as the second coming of Lincoln—or, really, just the second coming. His convincing win over GOP maverick John McCain was impressive. However, it was his cultlike following that caused many to believe he would rewrite the country's political DNA; that he was bigger than politics—bigger than the job he'd just won. Nobel Prizes were promptly awarded. Expectations for change were historic.

Then, something went wrong.

Barack Obama failed. He did not resuscitate the country's ailing economy. He maintained and even expanded the domestic spying policies of the Bush administration. His promises of openness and transparency went unfulfilled. Then, he pushed all his chips into the middle on Obamacare—a massive intergenerational con game, designed to pick the pockets of already struggling young Americans.

Many figured it out. Hope and change became fear and loathing. And Millennials became receptive to new arguments that transcended the big government Republicanism of George W. Bush and the big government liberalism of Barack Obama. Though Obama remains more popular among younger voters, he's managed to fall much, much farther—setting the stage for another political realignment.

Certainly, Millennials exhibit some core cultural traits that tend to favor the Left—and they probably always will. Examples include greater social tolerance, a taste for environmentalism, and a subtle sense of globalism. When it comes to making political decisions, the Millennial's left-leaning traits tend to manifest in the form of strong support for same-sex marriage, support for policies aimed at curbing climate change, and support for immigration reform.

However, Millennials also exhibit certain (underappreciated) core traits—some of which developed during the Great Recession—that ought to favor the Right, such as a strong sense of entrepreneurship, frugality, a penchant for personal choice, an inclination toward market-based competition and a distrust of large institutions, including government. The Millennial's right-leaning traits tend to manifest in the form of strong support for entitlement reform, including privatization and individual accounts, discomfort with deficit spending and growing skepticism of government's motives and effectiveness. Right-leaning traits can also be seen in the Millennial's strong personal choice ethic, which causes young majorities to support your right to guzzle giant sodas, smoke ecigarettes in public, gamble online, and munch on trans-fats as often as you desire (or your arteries can handle)—despite the protestations of progressives.[118]

Thus far, Millennials' left-leaning cultural traits have been in the ascendancy. You might say that Millennials have largely been social voters, not economic voters.

Writing for the *Daily Caller*, Milan Suri explains why: "We all have gay friends, but we haven't paid years of taxes yet."

That's changing (not the gay friends part but the taxes part). Although our public schools and post-secondary universities supply regular doses of liberalism, real life remains a crash course in conservatism. As Margaret Thatcher once famously observed, "the facts of life are conservative."

For the libertarian-leaning or fiscally-focused conservative, the opportunities to connect with young Americans quickly become apparent: The Millennial's underlying cultural feature is obsession with personal choice. Liberal dominance of our schools and media outlets have activated some of the Millennial's traditionally left-leaning personal choice instincts, leading them to adopt more liberal social positions on issues such as sex education, religion in schools, and same-sex marriage. The liberal did not instill these instincts in the Millennial—he merely awakened them; transformed them into political cues.

Similarly, conservatives need not instill fiscal conservatism in the Millennial—it is already there. The hardship of the Great Recession, the dearth of traditional employment, and the enormous weight of student loan debt have finely tuned the Millennial's bargain-hunting, penny-pinching instincts. In elections to come, smart conservative candidates will seek to awaken the Millennial's inherent sense of frugality and fiscal restraint and build their case around practical economics—replacing words like *voucher* with words like *choice* and swapping out words like *cut* with words like *budget*.

Third, *a change in the composition of the GOP:* Right now, the GOP and its candidates speak to those who constitute their coalition—mostly older, white voters. That's not a slight. It's just a fact. However, Millennials will eventually take the reigns of the Republican Party, just as they will inevitably exert greater influence on government and business. Although Millennials will be underrepresented within the GOP (at least at first), the sheer size of the generation will soon guarantee the rise of top candidates, donors, and party leaders from within its ranks.

Inevitably, the GOP will learn to speak the language of its new members. After all, that's what political parties do. The center of gravity within the party will begin to shift. By the 2020s, if not sooner, I expect that many social issues—namely same-sex marriage—will recede from the political spotlight. I do not know if this change will be memorialized within the party platform anytime soon, but that's not what matters. *Candidates* drive these debates. And libertarian-lite *candidates* will become increasingly common within the GOP.

Undoubtedly, the willingness of Millennials to discard traditional labels made them easy prey for Barack Obama, a generational candidate and once-persuasive peddler of statism. However, it works both ways. Smart conservative candidates will pitch free market solutions as part of a personal choice platform that, if delivered credibly and without pandering, will naturally appeal to Millennials.

In an age of declining political labels, expect a lot of the old *isms* to recede from the political dialogue, too. Communism, capitalism, and socialism—while relevant, these terms convey less direct meaning to Millennials than they did to previous generations. Perhaps it's because we're overeducated—we spent so much time in college classes hearing professors toss these terms around that they began to lose real meaning. Or perhaps it's because we're undereducated—we never fought communism or fascism and while we were raised to regard them as dangerous, we lack a practical, contemporary frame of reference for some of these terms.

Just like old school political buzzwords, Millennials are not animated by arguments based on the traditional clash between "capitalism" and "socialism." Partly, that's because an individual's view of "socialism" depends upon his personal understanding of what the term actually means. And that's a problem. Survey research indicates that only 30 percent of Americans can accurately define socialism. The rest are basing their opinion on incomplete or inaccurate information. Indeed, many will remember a 2012 poll in which a plurality of Millennials preferred socialism to capitalism. Yet, this appears to be another generational case of *lost in translation*. Once the term *socialism* is properly defined as a "government-managed economy" versus a "free market economy," support for socialism falls to 32 percent (in-line with the general population) and support for capitalism rises to 64 percent.[119]

At first, this generational language barrier may trouble conservatives. We don't want to give up our favorite words. And we tend to regard not only the principles of capitalism, but also *the word itself*, as somewhat sacrosanct. At a time when political correctness is running rampant, conservatives are often annoyed when their political leaders abandon the words that were once held in high esteem—putting "free market" in place of "capitalism," for example.

It's a credit to the conservative character that we fight for our words.

However, we must update our rhetoric if we expect to appeal to a new generation that uses a different vernacular. And before we dig in our heels on each and every antiquated term, we would do well to know where they came from in the first place.

Let's consider *capitalism* versus the *free market*, for example.

The first modern use of the word *capitalism* comes from Louis Blanc, a French socialist, and Pierre-Joseph Proudhon, a self-described anarchist. The word was popularized in Karl Marx's *Das Kapital.* So, before we cling too tightly to the *isms* we were raised on, let's first consider that these words were devised or, at a minimum, promoted, by those who sought to dismantle the free market.

I don't know about you, but personally, I prefer my terms of endearment to be ... you know, endearing. That's why the non-profit I represent is called *Free Market America* and not *Capitalism America.*

While Millennials are dumping many of the *isms*, I expect a lot of the *acracies* will go, too. Autocracies, technocracies, plutocracies, democracies; political scientists love to slice and dice these terms, but they tend to obscure rather than enhance the practical meaning behind our arguments. And 21st Century politics will be all about simplifying the complex.

Losing these labels may scare the shit out of conservatives. After all, we cherish our words. We learn from our history. We demand honest language from our leaders.

But conservatives are getting a better deal here. When you get rid of all the labels, when you simplify all the rhetoric, when you peel back this political onion to its philosophical core, all of the *isms* and all of the *acracies* fall into two simple boxes: Those that strengthen the *individual* and those that strengthen the *state*. Ultimately, there is no *acracy* or *ism*—there is only the *individual* and the *state*. The struggle between these two forces is ancient. It is the only truly meaningful distinction in all of political history. And it is on this basis that we must make our case.

In this increasingly simplified, Steve Jobs-style, label-light, ism-free world, politics will change. The convenient information shortcuts we use to describe political ideas, such as big government and socialism will be replaced with a new vernacular, or dropped altogether.

This will mean two things: First, in a world where "Republican" and "Democrat" means less, personal political brands will mean *more*. Second, politics will become more radical, less tethered to strict, traditional ideologies.

The old political pylons, with Reagan on the right and Clinton on the left, are gone. Heretofore unpopular, even inconceivable ideas, on both the Left and the Right, will be repackaged in populist boxes and given their day. Even as young Americans purport to crave the moderation of the middle, their aversion to party politics will ensure the nomination of increasingly partisan candidates. And freed from traditional political loyalties, Millennials will not hesitate to choose bold, aggressive change, if it's persuasively packaged and considered thoughtful, intelligent, and sincere.

As a result, we must discard old notions of what is radical.

Before this decade is out, fissures between the economic and social wings of the Republican Party will widen. Among Democrats, rifts between unions and environmentalists will widen, too, particularly as manufacturing mounts a comeback in the United States. Ideas once thought to belong solely to one end of the political spectrum will catapult to the other. There will be more *National Security Liberals* and *Anti-Spying Conservatives*, more *Pro-Life Democrats* and more *Pro-same sex Marriage Republicans*. Eventually, we may find ourselves inhabiting a political ecosystem in which ideologically unattached Millennials seesaw wildly between Leftwing and Rightwing populists as the country struggles to reach a new political equilibrium.

The risks will be high, the rewards great.

The Left will offer its own aggressive reforms, pitching voters the next logical level of statism—from private sector salary caps and single-payer healthcare rationing to truly troubling limits on free speech and property rights. They will prey on our worst instincts: Envy, anger, and fear.

For conservatives, this is no time for squishiness.

Surveys indicate that Millennials are *overwhelmingly* willing to entertain ideas that were once thought politically impractical, such as individual Social Security accounts and the replacement of Medicare's single-payer system. Young voters are clearly thirsty for a new model of government—but they don't know what it will look like. As a result, everything will be on the table—for both parties.

Voters will entertain once-unthinkable options. Who wins will depend on who can gore their own sacred cows first. Will Republicans tone down intense rhetoric on same-sex marriage and immigration before Democrats can discard antiquated attitudes toward entitlement spending and public employee unions?

No candidate has yet sated the nation's reemerging populist

appetite. Right now, it's anyone's game.

Not surprisingly, liberals are very excited that Millennials will eventually make up over a third of the electorate. They believe 2012 was the GOP's Waterloo; that conservatives are on the brink of extinction. When leftwing pundits look at the data, they are drawn to demographics; they are drawn to the newest generation's social liberalism. They conclude that they're on the right side of history.

Yes, they've seen the signs. But they've misread them.

Millennials have had front row seats to the grotesque dysfunction of Washington, with little evidence to suggest it will ever be different. Their handpicked government repairman, Barack Obama, once seemed poised to channel America's populist impulses but now demonstrates daily that he's not really equipped to unite a country or lead a great people. Over the long run, it is highly unlikely that Millennials will rubberstamp more government while simultaneously suspecting its motives, distrusting is methods and regarding it as incompetent.

By the late 2020s, the old entitlement state will be buckling under its own weight. The strain will be apparent. Millennials, who already appear to intuitively recognize that the old model of government is crumbling, will be receptive to reform—just as they are now. They have not grown accustomed to the old model, nor are they financially invested in it. Unlike their Depression-forged great grandparents, they have not seen government come to the rescue— they've seen it come to a halt. Their instincts, honed during the Bush-Obama years, will not be to double-down on the old model— because the old model is all about *Big. Distant. Statism.*

And *big* is out. *Small* is in. *Local* is in. *Individual* is in. A *Great Transition* in Washington is on the horizon.

In the coming decades—in a world where *big* is *bad*—the pivotal question will be: Whom do you trust? Conservatives must answer, "The individual." All the other *acracies* and *isms* are merely distinctions without a difference. Our bottom line: We stand for the individual.

And the other guys? They stand for the state.

THE TURNING POINT

CHAPTER 8
WINNERS WIN

Winners win.

And losers lose.

That's why successful presidents produce long-term majorities for their parties, while failed presidents produce long-term majorities for their opponents.

For example, Ronald Reagan's successful presidency created strong Republican majorities among late-wave Boomers and early-wave Gen-Xers—generations whose politics were forever shaped by the Gipper's successful two-term run. On the other hand, George W. Bush's unpopular presidency resulted in strong Democrat majorities among early-wave Millennials. Young voters, because they are in their formative political years, *react strongly* to whomever occupies the Oval.

Well, the results are in: Barack Obama is no Ronald Reagan.

In fact, President Obama appears to be tracing the unpopular path paved by George W. Bush. If this trend continues, history suggests that Obama's presidency will generate long-term conservative majorities among *late-wave* Millennials.

To understand why, let's travel back in time.

It's 1970.

President Nixon signs an extension of the 1965 Voting Rights Act requiring that 18 become the voting age in all federal, state, and local elections. A year later, Congress passes, and the states ratify, a constitutional amendment to that effect.

1972 is an election year.

Popular incumbent President Richard Nixon is seeking a second term. His Democrat opponent is South Dakota Senator George McGovern, widely known as an unabashed liberal. Nixon wins in a landslide, capturing 49 states and nearly 61 percent of the popular vote. His 18-million vote margin of victory is the largest in American history.

But Nixon's triumph is incomplete. Despite historic victories in the Electoral College, he fails to win some of America's newest voters. Whites between 18 and 24 years old side with McGovern and young voters end up among the few demographic cohorts that vote for McGovern in '72. [120]

Flash forward forty years. It's 2012.

The contrarian, formerly liberal white voters who once cast their lot with liberal lion George McGovern are now between 58 and 64 years old. They form one of the most reliably Republican voting blocs around and overwhelmingly prefer Mitt Romney to Barack Obama.[121]

Welcome back to 2014.

In this enlightened age of political data crunching, we still suffer from two dominant myths on politics and age. The first myth is that the politics of one's youth *remain* the politics of one's future; that onetime Democrats become lifetime Democrats. As our trip through time just revealed, that's not true. In fact, it's not even *close to true*. After picking McGovern over Nixon, young voters might easily have felt their choice validated by the Watergate scandal that engulfed Nixon's presidency in 1974. But they didn't. They moved rightward—a pattern we're beginning to observe among Millennials today. [122]

Which leads me to the second myth of politics and age—that of *inevitable* change.

While it is true that voters often become more conservative as they age, it is not *certain*. For example, Americans who turned 18 when FDR was in the White House were much more likely to vote Democrat than the rest of the population *throughout their lives*. Similarly, those who turned 18 when Ronald Reagan was president vote more Republican than the rest of the population.

The common factor here is *not* which party controlled the White House. The common factor is that both Ronald Reagan and Franklin Roosevelt were winners. Their time in office is, by and large, fondly remembered. Voters who came of age during their presidencies are more like to identify with their respective parties.

It works both ways.

Voters who came of age under the late stages of Richard Nixon's presidency are more likely to vote Democrat while those who came of age under the disastrous presidency of Jimmy Carter are more likely to vote Republican. As I said, winners *win* and losers *lose*.[123]

It's all about probabilities and tendencies. The notion that voters don't change their minds *is not* true. There's ample evidence to suggest that voter priorities can shift as new things become important, such as schools, retirement, and the tax burden. Typically, such changes are the result of *new experiences* activating *preexisting cultural features*, which had previously been politically dormant.

Similarly, the notion that voters forget their past is wrong, too. Americans who turn 18 under successful presidents are usually inclined to stick with that president's party later in life. However, Americans who turn 18 under unsuccessful presidents are likely to align with the opposition party later in life.

Put another way, if you liked your party, you keep it (and if you didn't, you don't).

When a presidency is a mixed bag (for example, Truman), it tends to produce mixed results over the long term. Voters are less likely to develop strong attachments to the party of the president in power during their formative voting years. There's no special brand loyalty or, for that matter, brand aversion.

As we've discussed, we're now witnessing the prospect of two, back-to-back, bipartisan, second-term presidential implosions—those of George W. Bush and Barack Obama. While Ronald Reagan and Bill Clinton enjoyed stable, even rising approval ratings at this point in their second terms, Barack Obama's numbers have followed the downward trajectory of his predecessor. Moreover, there's little to suggest that Obama's situation will improve. There's been no resolution of the alphabet-soup scandals at the IRS, NSA and VA and the president's only major legislative achievement, Obamacare, continues to torment ordinary Americans daily.

This is contributing to the rise of Independent voters, the widespread distrust of major parties, and the skepticism toward major institutions. At the same time, we're also getting a glimpse into the future. The last wave of Millennials—those who will cast their first presidential ballots in 2016 and 2020—are living through the failed presidency of Barack Obama. The impact of these soon-to-be voters will not be felt until after the Obama administration has ended.

However, the early signs are telling.

Older Millennials—those who came of age under President George W. Bush—leaned left. However, it seems that *younger* Millennials—those coming of age under Barack Obama—are trending more conservative. 42 percent of 18 and 19 year olds consider themselves conservative—slightly higher than the population at large and significantly higher than early-wave Millennials. Only about a third of these late-wavers say they are liberal. That's nearly the mirror-opposite of older Millennials.[124]

Writing for *The Guardian*, Harry Enten points out that this trend approximates the one that preceded the *Reagan Revolution* in 1980. Between 2008 and 2012, liberal identification among first-year college men and women fell by 4 and 5 points, respectively—bringing them in line with the more moderate college freshman of the Carter and Clinton years. While there are more self-identified liberals today than there were during the Reagan presidency, the *decline* among self-identified college-age liberals is "nearly on par with what occurred between 1976 and 1980." [125]

Among Millennials as a whole, liberals still edge out conservatives. However, among *younger* Millennials in 4-year colleges, conservatives edge out liberals. Younger Millennials are also less likely to approve of the way Barack Obama is handling the economy, budget deficits, or healthcare. They're more likely to believe tax cuts spark economic growth, more likely to support school choice, and more likely to say energy independence should be a priority than older Millennials.[126]

Let's go even younger.

In both 2004 and 2008, high school students supported John Kerry and Barack Obama at roughly the same rate as 18 to 24 year-olds. Put another way, the generation was politically monolithic. However, this changed *dramatically* in 2012, when high school students became 21-points less likely to back Obama than college-age Millennials. [127] And all of this predates the IRS, NSA and VA scandals, as well as the Obamacare nightmare—which has sent the president's support among young voters to new lows.

Among older, early-wave Millennials, George W. Bush and Barack Obama form the two pylons of political memory. These voters associate George W. Bush with the Great Recession, soaring debt, and two costly foreign wars. Most can remember neither a successful Republican presidency nor a successful Democrat presidency. Even though their enthusiasm has waned and their support has diminished, they still prefer Barack Obama to most GOP alternatives.

On the other hand, younger Millennials—those between 18 and 24 years of age—are more conservative. The unsuccessful presidency of George W. Bush does not really fall within their political memory. So, what are the twin pylons of *their* political experience?

Candidate Obama and *President* Obama.[128]

They remember the cultish fervor that surrounded his first coronation ... ahem, election; they remember the slow-motion misery that ensued. For these new Millennials, the president's failure to meet—or even approach—the expectations he set serves as the signature political event of their lives. Unless things improve for President Obama, these younger Millennials may end up voting less like their older siblings and more like their Gen-X predecessors—that is to say, *more conservative*.

So, it turns out that the best cure for Obama is...Obama.

Many on the Left believe Millennials are too staunchly Democratic to ever reconsider their political loyalties. However, that's just not true. Millennials are actually *less* Democratic than Boomers, Silents and members of the GI Generation were at similar ages. For example, 45 percent of Silents considered themselves Democrats in 1956. Compare that to 2008—by all accounts a blowout year for the Left—when only 41 percent of Millennials considered themselves Democrats.[129]

It's not just Eisenhower-era Silents. Young Boomers were not only *more* Democratic they were also *less* Republican than Millennials. In 1974, only 17 percent of Boomers considered themselves Republicans while 47 percent—nearly 3-to-1—considered themselves Democrats. Compare that with the 22 percent of Millennials who described themselves as Republicans in 2008.[130]

Yes, Millennials are more racially diverse than older generations, which typically points to stronger liberalism. However, younger Hispanics are 9-points less likely to consider themselves Democrats than older Hispanics.[131] This might be explained by the fact that most Hispanics under 30 were born in the United States, whereas most Hispanics over 30 were board abroad. Not surprisingly, this younger Hispanic cohort prefers to speak mostly or solely English in their everyday lives, unlike their older counterparts, for whom Spanish predominates.[132]

Moreover, on key metrics, Millennials mirror the population at large. Millennials' views of business and profits are in line of that with other generations. Some might even say they're more favorable to business, with 44 percent of Millennials agreeing that "business corporations generally strike a fair balance between making profits and serving the public interest," compared to only 35 percent of Gen-Xers and Boomers and 32 percent of Silents.[133] At the same time, solid majorities of young voters now agree government is "usually inefficient and wasteful," that federal agencies routinely abuse their power and that businesses are paying their fair share of taxes.[134]

Additionally, though they were less skeptical of government in 2008, Millennials were no more likely than Boomers to favor a wider social safety net. Since then, Millennials' support for all things big, government included, continues to decline. [135]

While Democrats are busy imbibing their own *Coalition of the Ascendant* Kool-Aid (with too many conservatives glumly joining them), let's do a little forecasting.

At around 65-years old (and with roughly 20 solid voting years to go), the dependably Republican Boomer is entering what *RealClearPolitics'* Sean Trende calls the "peak voting years." Over the next two decades, early-wave Millennials will continue to shed some of their liberalism while late-wave Millennials—though socially moderate—may emerge as a potent force for fiscal conservatism. By 2035, this generation will have followed the Boomers' winding path to the right.

By the late 2020s and the early 2030s, this convergence of right-trending Millennials and still-standing Boomers may very well produce a surprising turnabout in national elections. Democrats may find they can no longer count on an outsized share of the fickle, brand-averse Millennial vote, while Boomers remain a healthy, viable, and overrepresented Republican base well into the future.

Of course, Barack Obama's failures will only take us so far.

The winner of the White House in 2016 will have an outsized influence on the Millennials' final phase of formative political education. Will we become increasingly conservative, as Boomers have? Or will we become a mixed bag—a tossup generation, like those who come of age during nothing-burger presidencies or back-to-back bipartisan letdowns? There's no way to know for certain. However, the stage is set for a charismatic, conservative candidate to capitalize on late-wave Millennial angst as well as broader populist appetites and do what Barack Obama could not:

Win a generational victory.

CHAPTER 9
AMERICAN PHOENIX

"Let me tell you what's going to happen to government and politics when *we* get ahold of them. We'll destroy them." [136]

Yikes.

That's Shayan, a whip-smart Langley High senior and a Millennial. His comment—made to Ron Fournier at *The Atlantic*—might be taken as anarchism, if not for what he said next: "The thing about social institutions is when you destroy them, they get rebuilt eventually, in a different form for a different time." [137]

He's right.

A late-wave Millennial, Shayan seems to instinctively understand that something is shifting in the shadows. Somewhere along the way, those old Industrial Age institutions, which had hummed along happily since the Great Depression, stopped working. Lately, Washington has pulled every lever and pushed every button, trying desperately to engineer the economic and social outcomes it desires. It tried to boost homeownership and plug college attendance; it tried to mandate healthcare and create fictitious energy markets; it even tried to tell us how much soda we should drink, which light bulbs we can use, and what cars we could drive.

The more they failed, the harder they tried.

However, the inadequacy of old institutions became dreadfully clear when the market crashed in 2008. Looking back, it's easy to see the writing was on the wall. Like a horse-drawn carriage trying to keep pace with a car, government struggled to keep up with a world that had grown more complex. Every button Washington pushed flipped a hundred switches somewhere else, triggering a cascade of unintended consequences and wreaking untold damage to the economy. But Washington didn't repent of its button-pushing ways. On the contrary, every failure seemed like an excuse to push *even harder*.

Remarkably, when the housing bubble burst there were *seven* agencies ostensibly tasked with looking after this sector of the economy: The Federal Housing Administration, the Federal National Mortgage Association (better known as Fannie Mae), the Government National Mortgage Association (better known as Ginnie Mae), the Federal Home Loan Mortgage Corporation (better known as Freddie Mac), the Neighborhood Reinvestment Corporation, the Federal Housing Finance Board and the Office of Federal Housing Enterprise Oversight.[138]

For the last century, we've been hatching new government agencies to protect us from economic downturns. Yet, we've had a Great Depression, a Great Recession and countless other dips and dives in between. These obvious failures have not prevented government from meddling. "The more the plans fail," noted Ronald Reagan, "the more the planners plan."

An innovation-economy is far too complex for factory-style economic engineering. Information is too diffused. People are too different. Things change too quickly. Government simply *cannot* do it all; it cannot possibly predict the near-infinite outputs produced by a handful of top-down inputs. Fostered by technology and the fragmentation of traditional media, there are now more people with unique opinions and diverse desires than government could ever hope to manage wisely. And Industrial Age government is a slow-moving tank; it's not built for speed or tight curves.

Government must grow up. And that will mean slimming down.

Though still maturing themselves, Millennials seem destined to preside over this change. In the next few decades, they will find their way into the old institutions and *rebuild them*, as Shayan said, "in a different form for a different time." As Millennials take the reigns, we'll begin to leave behind the slapdash adolescence of the last 25 years; to devise a new model for government, based on the recognition that its powers are limited, if no longer in theory, then certainly in reality.

Fortunately, a *new model* is already in production. 2035 is the year to watch.

Mark it on your calendar.

Well, don't actually mark it on your calendar. That would be ridiculous. But, you know, keep it in your head, okay? I'm going to set out a plausible scenario that takes us through 2035. Nothing is written in stone and, certainly, any number of intervening variables could upset the particulars. However, the fundamentals are sound.

This scenario is based on what we know of political history, what we've learned of Millennials' culture and politics, and what we can see of the economic and geopolitical trends shaping America's future. Hang tight.

We will end where we began, with the *Five Pillars of American Power:*

The first and most important of the *Five Pillars* is *Economic Dynamism.* The true wellspring of American prosperity, *Economic Dynamism* is a powerful combination of free enterprise, creative destruction, industry diversity, market depth, and high productivity. Unlike the stagnant superpowers of the past, the American economy seldom stands still. It is constantly being reborn, constantly creating new markets and new industries. Hard work and entrepreneurship are typically celebrated and rewarded. The individual is at the center of economic life. Without a doubt, this pillar was cracked by the Great Recession and nearly toppled by the Obama administration's mindless efforts to manage economic outcomes from Washington. However, *Economic Dynamism* is driven by the notion of *choice*—a core value for America, and one that is central to Millennials and the century they will soon come to dominate.

The second pillar is *Domestic Stability*, which deals with matters such as the Rule of Law, healthy population growth and the orderly operation of society. America's *Domestic Stability* has suffered due to the events immediately preceding and following the Great Recession. These events are a direct result of antiquated policymaking, fostered by command-and-control-style economic planning out of Washington. However, as I'll soon explain, the forthcoming *Great Transition* will produce entitlement reform, an immigration overhaul and substantial change in how government operates—all with significant implications for *Domestic Stability*.

The third pillar is *Cultural Universality*, which encompasses the many intangibles that contribute to America's appeal abroad. Recently, this pillar suffered from a combination of unpopular foreign adventures during the Bush era and, on the flipside of the coin, craven weakness during the Obama years. Nonetheless, a return to America's core value of *personal freedom* combined with the growing consumerism of the developing world and a changing geopolitical landscape will strengthen America's alliances and boost *Cultural Universality*.

The fourth pillar is *Military Primacy*, which is directly tied to *Economic Dynamism.* The national defense is funded by government, which is funded by tax revenues, which depend upon economic prosperity. In recent years, the Department of Defense has suffered serious budget cuts. At the same time, China has invested heavily in modernizing its military. Fortunately, the US advantage in this arena is significant enough that the Obama administration cannot undo it single-handedly. In addition, the US is not the only nation that is skeptical of China's regional ambitions. The next generation will have ample opportunity to strengthen the American alliance system and confront a rising China in the Pacific.

The fifth pillar, *Energy Security,* deals with the fuel that powers our economy and our lives. Without a doubt, the Obama administration has attempted to undermine the quest for energy independence by seeking to regulate traditional fuels out of existence. But it has failed. The free market has proven resilient. The United States is now well positioned for energy independence for the first time in a long time. Once achieved, energy independence will support *Economic Dynamism* by reducing domestic manufacturing costs. At the same time, no longer hamstrung by its foreign energy addiction, the US will enjoy greater flexibility in foreign affairs, strengthening *Military Primacy.*

While the next few years will be tough, the next two decades will ultimately strengthen the *Five Pillars of American Power.* Specifically, *five major events* will unfold. Together, these events will create the conditions necessary for a major *Turning Point—* something of a reversal in our recent national fortunes.

The First Event: America's *Three Cultural Drivers—* entertainment, the news media, and education—will undergo extensive fragmentation. Yeah, I know that sounds really bad. And if you're a liberal, it is. But for the conservative, this is the closest thing you get to a political panacea. This fragmentation, brought about largely by technology, will reset the proverbial chessboard, boost conservative influence in the media, and pave the way for structural reform to government. While this will cause short-term damage to *Domestic Stability* it will, in the long run, fortify all *Five Pillars of American Power.*

The Second Event: Millennials' rightward drift, if not really a Republican drift, will nonetheless set the stage for a decade of more fiscally conservative politics shaped by Millennials and Boomers. This *new politics* will defy traditional labels; it will incline heavily toward personal choice—meaning social moderation, fiscal conservatism, and a strain of tech-populism. The crowning political achievement of this *new politics* will likely occur in the 2020s, when America's unsustainable entitlement system will finally undergo reform, strengthening *Domestic Stability* and *Economic Dynamism.*

The Third Event: No sooner will America tame its debt demons than our chief geopolitical rival, China, will begin to face demographic challenges that border on the catastrophic. At the same time, economic and social convulsions within China may position the United States favorably, strengthening both *Military Primacy* and *Economic Dynamism.* However, it is possible China's convulsions will be so severe that the country becomes an economic and political basket case, with serious repercussions for the US and the world. Regardless, this is the only *major event* that will be shaped as much (or more) by the decisions of foreign leaders as by the choices of Americans themselves.

The Fourth Event: As the developed world faces labor shortages, international competition for the best and the brightest will grow fierce. However, a series of sensible updates to our immigration system—aimed at strengthening and modernizing border security while promoting increased *legal* immigration—will enable the United States to compete aggressively for new talent, averting population decline, and ensuring healthy, stable economic growth.

The Fifth Event: The United States will emerge from years of political turmoil confident, secure, and energy independent. While Millennials' libertarian-tinged foreign policy outlook may invite future conflict, America's robust domestic energy supply will bolster *Energy Security* and power a minor manufacturing renaissance, setting the stage for stable GDP growth on the order of 3 to 4 percent.

Let's tackle each of these *major events,* one-at-a-time:

The Three Cultural Drivers

"We have shaped a world culture through you," President Obama told members of the entertainment industry.

I don't make a habit of agreeing with Barack Obama—but he's right...this once.

Fortune 500 companies, major industry groups, top political candidates and countless others spend nearly $64 billion annually on TV to shape public attitudes, drive consumer behavior and, some might say, elect presidents.[139] The medium is so powerful, so effective that advertisers spend billions to share their message with consumers in tiny 30-second increments.

I'm tired of hearing the words, "It's just a TV show" to excuse the overtly liberal themes that often drive traditional television programming. If 30-second ads are powerful enough to alter consumer behavior, shape public opinion, and put presidents in the White House—imagine the power of a 30-*minute* TV show.

Why, it'd be enough to impact the culture of a nation.

While politicians tinker on society's margins, the entertainment industry is repainting the picture. For decades, the Left has largely controlled what appears on our televisions and in our movie theaters. So, it's no surprise that environmental extremism has surged, liberal social values have flourished, and our notions of good and evil have been all-but deconstructed. To some extent, even our patriotism has waned.

Too often, it seems that when conservatives get their hands on a camera and a budget, we make movies, documentaries, and TV programs that deliver heavy-handed sermons—not entertainment. We're so rarely given the reigns of a major entertainment property that we get overexcited when we fall ass-backward into an opportunity. We cram our ideology, our *message*, into every second of the program. We try to force-feed conservatism to people who are paying for entertainment. And it doesn't work.

If there's one-thing conservatives should know it's that moviegoers and TV-watchers can sense a sermon a mile away. After all, *we* do. Remember all of those terrible anti-war movies churned out during the Bush years? Hollywood couldn't help itself—it just *had* to protest. These silly sermonettes were almost always flops. But liberal producers, writers, directors, and actors simply *could not imagine* that the rest of America did not share their convictions, their sense of near-constant outrage. So they made movie after movie that no one wanted to see. It was ridiculous.

Well, we've made the same mistake—with much less margin for error.

We've put ideology above entertainment and we often forget that people go to the movies and watch TV to be *entertained*. The opportunity for persuasion arises only once entertainment has been accomplished. Conservative moviemakers and TV writers ought to make films and programs that satisfy the market's desire for *entertainment*. The message—the politics—can come secondly, and therefore, more seductively. The virtues of competition, the absurdity of environmentalism, the rank incompetence of government, the heroism of the small business owner—all of these themes and more could easily be insinuated into entertainment properties without aggressive moralizing.

Sure, Shangri-La sounds great. But how will we get there?

Our journey is already underway. It began with the convergence of television and the Internet. Today, I can watch most network and cable programming online as well on TV. After all, both mediums are merely delivery platforms for video content. The convergence of these mediums, combined with the fragmentation of entertainment offerings—first exemplified by the rise of cable—will offer conservatives opportunities to enter the entertainment marketplace as never before.

Once upon a time, networks only produced TV shows for which they already had a timeslot. But what if timeslots disappear altogether? The rise of on demand programming, from Hulu to Netflix to iTunes, offers new venues for content that is *not* bound by traditional timeslot constraints. Already, third parties can produce and market content to on demand providers without worrying when it will run.

This flexible future will afford conservative writers, directors, producers, and actors greater opportunities to write entertainment content and pitch movie concepts. But more importantly, the great leveling tool of our time—the Internet—will allow conservative creators to deliver entertainment (and, when they're not looking, a message) to the millions of Americans who are increasingly seeking information, news, and entertainment outside of established channels.

Historically, liberals have controlled entertainment only because it *could* be controlled. That's changing. Sure, it's not going to be easy for conservatives to make waves in entertainment. But it's going to be *easier* than it was before.

The walls of the big studios are crumbling. The production barriers and heavy capital requirements are disintegrating. The entertainment complex in Hollywood cannot control the vast and growing sphere of *new* entertainment, which lives online and will, inevitably, spread to other outlets as well. Technology, once again, is fragmenting the old order—eroding traditional entertainment institutions and dividing viewership. As the Left's entertainment monopoly collapses, conservatives will find themselves with new opportunities to shape the entertainment world.

And it's not just entertainment.

The Left's uncontested control of the news media has already ended. The first major chink in the armor appeared in the mid-90s, when media pioneer Roger Ailes proved the existence of a vast, rightwing...marketplace. For decades, conservatives and even-tempered moderates couldn't stomach their dinners while also trying to stomach the six o'clock news. Thus, Fox. And today, the top thirteen programs on cable news are on the Fox News Channel.[140]

Of course, the largest and most untamed news space is the Internet.

At first, conservatives lagged behind liberals when it came to understanding and using the power of this highly shareable medium. That's no longer the case. Led by Matt Drudge, a cadre of online bloggers and commentators reshaped this space. From Michelle Malkin to Tucker Carlson to Andrew Breitbart and numerous others, conservative exiles fleeing traditional news media outlets brought about something of a conservative renaissance within the walls of this new, digital world.

Meanwhile, an eclectic mix of media entrepreneurs and political talkers—from Rush Limbaugh to Glenn Beck to Mark Levin—have made and remade the conservative talk radio project every election cycle. Rush launched the medium decades ago, pioneering a new, anti-establishment brand of conservative radio, literature, and even TV. Others followed. More recently, Glenn Beck expanded his work into various online news properties, including TheBlaze and TheBlaze TV—which incorporate a variety of on-air talent.

Conservatives are no longer seeking to quietly infiltrate the old bastions of liberal news reporting. Instead, they're seeking to replace them. As a result, the profession of journalism is in a state of flux. And I'm not just talking about the abundance of empty newsrooms, the decline of old school reporting, or even the bankruptcy of notable newspapers. I'm talking about the *decline* of hard news.

Amazon founder, Jeff Bezos, rescued the sinking *Washington Post*. Media giants like *ESPN, Bloomberg, Reuters*, and the *Wall Street Journal* all cater to specific markets and carry mostly niche or commercial news, for which their readers happily pay. With a handful of exceptions, there is little consumer appetite for *paid* national news. What about the *New York Times*? *The Times* now receives more revenue from its subscribers, than from advertisers— a sign, says *Reuters* columnist Jack Shafer, that subscribers "value [*The Times'*] mission more than Madison Avenue does."[141]

But with consumers increasingly unwilling to *pay* for national hard news (something they've always gotten as a freebie), the question becomes: What will take its place?

The answer: *A lot of things.*

By the 2030s, we'll still have *local* hard news, for which readers and viewers seem willing to pay. Similarly, niche publications like *Politico* will satisfy the Washington chattering classes while national publications like *The Wall Street Journal* continue to feed a financial clientele. However, with many news outlets operating on thinner margins, it is unlikely they will continue to offer robust national hard news coverage, which is not much of a revenue-generator.

It's also unlikely that major media outlets can continue to count on philanthropists, like Bezos, to step in and bail them out. Instead, it seems that the thing most likely to *replace* national hard news is national news *commentary*. Unlike its hard news cousin, commentary can be quite profitable, both because consumers desire it and because it is less expensive to produce. [142]

Understandably, many conservatives will celebrate the decline of old-school media outlets. After all, liberal media's hard news bears a striking resemblance to political commentary anyway. Let's set aside the debate on whether this is good or bad for news for civil debate (the Left's term for one-sided bloviating that masquerades as objectivity) and instead consider what it means for our politics.

The waning of traditional media is a net loss for liberals because there are presently more liberal journalists than conservative journalists. Suppose the Left controls roughly 90 percent of the news media but nowhere near 90 percent of the electorate. As news options are increasingly customized to the user, the politics behind those options will come to roughly reflect the views of the electorate itself—more of a 50/50 split. For the Left, which is accustomed to dominating this space, it will feel a lot like having the board reset when you're on the verge of victory.[143]

This development will change the political environment for conservatives.

Just look at the data. Economists Stefano DellaVigna and Ethan Kaplan found that George W. Bush's vote share increased nearly half-a-percent in areas where Fox News was available.[144] Similarly, Yale researchers discovered that a Democrat candidate's vote total was nearly 4-points higher among *Washington Post* subscribers than subscribers to the more conservative *Washington Times*.[145] Is this because *Washington Post* readers became more liberal or because liberals tend to prefer the *Washington Post*? It's probably a bit of both. One thing is certainly clear: Pointy-headed academics of various backgrounds seem to believe that the partisan makeup of the news media influences the outcome of elections.

By the 2030s, we'll see news outlets that look a lot like they're from the ... *1830s*.

Bloomberg's Megan McArdle posits that the funding gap for hard news will invite big donors and political parties back into the news industry. "Back" is the key word. The notion of partisan newspapers is not new. Quite the contrary, for most of our nation's history news outlets had a distinctly partisan hue. It's only in recent generations that the myth of media objectivity took root.[146]

McArdle notes that, "ideological media will probably also be a more conservative" because there are more conservative donors and viewers than there are conservative media moguls. As a result, the liberals' "edge will probably slip." And while Democrat candidates enjoy an advantage from having the traditional news media space all to their own, "that edge will probably get smaller in the future." [147]

While the Left's media monopoly is ending, its iron-fisted grip on the third *Cultural Driver*—education—is slowly loosening, too.

The rise of charter schools and the proliferation of non-traditional online colleges are changing the way people acquire an education. At the same time, support for parent choice and merit pay is rising. Almost certainly, Democrats will have an even tougher time navigating the rough waters that will surely ensue when two rock-solid Democrat constituencies—the Teachers Unions and African American voters—clash over the simmering school choice debate.

Unions may not survive another generation of debate on school choice. Amidst highly publicized union battles taking place in New Jersey and Wisconsin, a mere 22 percent of Americans said that unions have a positive effect on our nation's schools. Meanwhile, only 43 percent of teachers held a positive view of their own unions—down from 58 percent in 2011. This may explain the roughly 150,000 teachers who cancelled their NEA membership in 2011 and 2012. The union anticipates that it will lose another 200,000 before 2015, as some states eliminate the automatic dues deductions from teacher paychecks.[148] A recent national poll of union households indicates that a third would terminate their union membership if given the chance. And increasingly, state legislatures are doing just that.[149]

In the short-term, fragmentation of the *Three Cultural Drivers* will lead to incivility and, potentially, unrest. The decline of hard news means voters will increasingly operate with different sets of facts. Partisanship may rise as a result. Political donors and parties may even invest in their own media outfits, too. If that happens, ideological divisions will sharpen. This will damage *Domestic Stability*. However, fragmentation will also democratize the news, create choices, and establish a framework that better reflects the voting preferences of the people. Ultimately, that's good for *Domestic Stability*—even if it produces short-term disruptions.

Moreover, media fragmentation will steadily improve political conditions for conservative reformers and lay the groundwork for domestic policies that strengthen both *Military Primacy* and *Economic Dynamism*. By the 2020s, fragmentation of the *Three Cultural Drivers* will loosen the Left's vicelike grip on American culture. Without these powerful institutions constantly delivering subtle doses of liberalism, conservatives will finally have room to breathe and, occasionally, drive the debate. At the same time, liberals' margin for error will narrow, as their long-time media allies' share of the total news audience continues to shrink. The end of the monolithic media establishment will embolden political reformers to tackle once-intractable issues, including entitlement reform.

Debt & Entitlement Reform

The cause of entitlement reform will be buoyed by a more conservative news climate. And thanks to the fragmentation of the *Three Cultural Drivers*, that is exactly what we will get. However, by itself, fragmentation will not be sufficient to fix America's crushing debt problem, begging the question: What great travesty of liberalism could possibly make the politics of entitlement reform *work*? Surely, it would first require a colossal failure of the welfare state to give impetus to lasting, structural reform of Social Security and Medicare? Well, funny you should ask.

On the PBS *NewsHour*, Democrat pundit Mark Shields hints at the answer:

"This is beyond the Obama Administration. If this goes down [...] if the Affordable Care Act is deemed a failure, this is the end [...] of liberal government. The public confidence in that will be so depleted, so diminished, that I really think [...] the equation of American politics changes."[150]

Mark's got it right.

President Obama bet the farm on the Affordable Care Act (ACA) and used the central conceit of liberalism—the idea that big government can solve big problems—as collateral. Now, the entire ideology is bankrupt.

It won't get better for them. It'll get worse.

The first wave of Obamacare-induced policy cancellations in the individual market caused chaos and outrage. But it's only the tip of the iceberg. President Obama can attempt to dismantle his eponymous law piece-by-piece or unilaterally delay the pain until after the midterms. But eventually, either another wave of cancellations will strike or the law's structural supports will begin to crumble. Already, the economics of Obamacare are atrocious—with most of those insured via the Affordable Care Act receiving federal subsidies while the administration simultaneously prepares for the possible bail out of insurance companies.

Left-leaning pundits enthusiastically tout ACA enrollment figures that, at the time of the law's passage, would have been considered miserably weak. That Obamacare is now a smoldering wreck instead of a raging engine fire should not be cause for celebration. Particularly since the fact remains: Unless the president lawlessly dismantles his only legislative achievement, the second wave of policy cancellations will be much, much larger than the first. The American Enterprise Institute, the Federal Register, and the Obama administration itself estimate that roughly 75 million Americans with employer-sponsored insurance would have lost their plans by the end of 2014 had the president not unilaterally delayed these cancellations. Some estimates put the number as high as 100 million.[151] That's 20 times greater than the first wave, so you can easily imagine the chaos.

Perhaps the best explanation of Obamacare's problems—and government's 21st Century challenge—comes from Blake Sisney, healthy, 27-year old Millennial:

"If it's such a great thing, how come they have to force it on me?"[152]

Good question, Blake. Turns out it was never a good idea anyway. It was always a relic from a bygone era when big entitlements defined Washington's contribution to society, when byzantine Industrial Age bureaucracies staffed by legions of federal workers were the norm. But that age is ending. Obamacare is not the beginning of a new dawn of liberalism—it is its dying gasp. The failure of the Affordable Care Act not only threatens to unravel itself; it has created deep doubt in the workability of the welfare state. It's also set the table for broad-based entitlement reform that may even include market-based competition in Medicare and personal accounts in Social Security. If conservatives are smart, they will use the opportunity of Obamacare to advance the conversation on entitlement reform, not retreat from it.

Ultimately, *three pivotal developments* will spark meaningful reform.

The first pivotal development: In 2018, scheduled increases in Social Security and Medicare spending will cause deficits to begin rising once more. Soon, Americans will once again face trillion-dollar annual shortfalls. Not surprisingly, public concern over the national debt tends to increase when deficits increase. As a result, the inevitable debate on entitlement reform will take place in the context of rising federal spending, trillion-dollar deficits and growing public concern over debt.

The second pivotal development: By 2020, debt-conscious Millennials will constitute nearly 40 percent of the electorate. While they are certainly not Republicans, they are not reliable Democrats either. With half now calling themselves Independents and with late-wave Millennials trending more conservative, this generation is on the path to become a "tossup" group sometime in the 2020s. Study after study makes clear that this build-your-own-playlist, design-your-own-sneakers and flavor-your-own-soda generation does not feel bound by traditional political dichotomies, such as Republican and Democrat. They are perfectly happy to hopscotch between parties and support an eclectic mix of ideas that defy rigid Left-Right categorization.[153]

Due to their size and political free agency, candidates will be forced to compete aggressively for Millennials' support. Although there are few issues on which this generation can agree, greater *personal choice* is among them. That's why Millennials overwhelmingly support personal Social Security accounts and market-based competition in Medicare, to the tune of 86 and 74 percent respectively.[154] Candidates will (eventually) take notice.

The third pivotal development: Entitlement reform will be packaged differently. Traditionally, Americans agree on only one thing when it comes to the national debt: *It's a problem.* Unfortunately, specific solutions usually fail to garner widespread support. Republicans favor cuts. Democrats favor tax hikes. Independents favor neither—but, of course, still want a solution. This led many to conclude that the debt crisis simply cannot be solved—that the problem is intractable and that our political leaders will, therefore, lack the guts to undertake real reform.

The figures are daunting: A slim 34 percent of voters back piecemeal Medicare and Social Security reforms.[155] But that's not the whole story. Everyone's heard the phrase, "misery loves company." Well, it's true. And, put simply, people tend to think of debt reduction as misery. No one wants to suffer its ill effects alone. That's why, when considered independently, Americans generally oppose most entitlement reform measures, such as raising the retirement age, raising Medicare's eligibility age, means testing, raising Medicare contributions, eliminating various tax deductions, and so forth.

The reasons are selfish, but simple.

However, there's a practical path home: *Merge* entitlement reform with tax reform and other spending cuts—and do it all at once. Voter support for chained CPI, gradual increases to the Medicare eligibility age, means testing, and similar steps all approach or exceed *60 percent* when combined with the elimination of various tax loopholes and reductions in government waste.[156]

Most voters—including most Republicans—overwhelmingly support Medicare and Social Security. They view them as "part of the deal" for Middle Class America. They resent government excess. They distrust politicians and bureaucrats. And they don't want to see the *their deal* undercut while the excesses of others are ignored. Generally speaking, Middle Class Americans are willing to feel the pain—but they don't want to feel it alone. I suppose you could call this the "everyone suffers" plan.

At the end of the day, entitlement reform was never going to be a walk in the park. However, a combination of more favorable media conditions, rising deficit fears, reform-minded, debt-sensitive Millennials, and a gradual, comprehensive approach that ties spending cuts to tax reform renders that which was once considered politically impossible, suddenly *doable.*

The resolution of this seemingly intractable issue will boost American confidence, shore up declining faith in the dollar and, by effect, strengthen *Cultural Universality.* It will also free up capital for private investment, put the United States on a stable path to growth and by extension, strengthen *Economic Dynamism.*

America's resolution of its debt crisis will also enable modest increases in military spending, which are needed to reinforce US *Military Primacy,* support Asia-Pacific allies and counter a potentially aggressive China. At the same time, entitlement reform will improve our debt-to-GDP ratio, enable greater flexibility in foreign affairs, and strengthen our geopolitical position vis-à-vis China in the 2020s and 2030s.

Taming the Dragon

With its burgeoning economy, modernized military, and tidy share of American debt, China is something of a modern boogeyman. It keeps us up at night.

However, before China aroused American anxieties, Japan was the object of our fears. Before Japan, it was the Soviet Union. In fact, US economists in the 1960s projected the Soviet economy would overtake our own by the year 2000.[157] Of course, the Soviet empire collapsed long before that could happen. Likewise, Japan's bubble burst and the country never quite mended. What will be China's fate?

One way or another, America's Millennials will confront this dragon.

It is unclear, however, if they will confront a destabilized China that threatens the global economy or a unified China that threatens American military power. In any case, our relationship with China is now the most important in the world. Unquestionably, how we manage that relationship will have enormous implications for each of the *Five Pillars of American Power.*

However, contrary to popular belief, China is afflicted by problems that are many, deep-seeded, and multivariate. Its top three challenges are *demographics, debt* and, because I'm sticking with the whole "D" thing here, *dumb*—meaning its economy is dumb, rather than dynamic. I'll explain.

China's *first challenge* is its most counterintuitive: Not enough people.

Despite a population of more than 1.3 billion, China faces a potentially catastrophic population crash in the next several decades. Its total fertility rate is 1.55—well below the 2.1 replacement rate required to maintain population stability. Like most developed countries, the United States also has a lower fertility rate, but it compensates with historically strong immigration, bringing its numbers in line with replacement rates, at about 2.06.[158]

We're lucky. Without stable population growth, the costs associated with caring for the elderly become an enormous burden on a dwindling workforce. Taxes, spending, and debt soar. Funding for growth-oriented projects, such as education, suffer. Such a demographic catastrophe would be deeply destabilizing, so much so that it can redraw maps and create new geopolitical realities. Traditionally, strong immigration has enabled the United States to avoid this fate, which would quickly bring about the collapse of the *Five Pillars of American Power*, beginning with *Economic Dynamism* and ending with *Domestic Stability.*

Soon, however, China will face *exactly* this problem.

Within the next decade, China's elderly population will begin to climb dramatically. By the 2030s, it will start to experience the first signs of economic slowdown, heralding a mid-century population collapse, in which nearly a third of its people will be over 60-years old.[159] That's demographic poison, which bodes doubly ill for a country that will be trying to manage a Herculean transition from export-based economy to consumer-based economy.

To make matters worse, China's brutal and backward attitudes on gender have set the stage for yet another serious social crisis. Thanks to the widespread abortion of unborn girls, there are roughly 118 newborn boys for every 100 newborn girls. At the moment, this is tragic. By the 2030s, when nearly a sixth of the country's adult men are unable to find spouses, it will spawn serious social unrest. At the same time, the country will be struggling to absorb soaring healthcare and pension costs associated with its rapidly rising senior population, easily dwarfing those of the United States.[160]

China's internal figures, which project 6 percent economic growth in 2020, do not fully account for the its looming demographic crisis. Factoring in demographic trends, the US Conference Board projects the Peoples' Republic will grow at a more subdued rate of 3.7 percent in 2020. At the same time, America could very well be flying high on its own domestic energy boom and growing at similar levels. [161]

Even the most eminent US pessimists are calling attention to China's questionable accounting. "If you adjust Chinese GDP for environmental degradation and for over-investment in things that will never be used, it falls in size by 30 to 50 percent," says economist Clyde Presotwitz, a noted US declinist. "Much of this would show up as non-performing loans in most economies but since such loans are never recognized in China, it will show up as slower growth in future years." [162]

Dangerous demographics? No biggie. Faulty figures? Oh, well. China's got a much more immediate threat—one that may bite it in the ass before the decade is out.

Debt. And not *our* debt.

That's China's *second challenge.* Citing "underlying structural weaknesses," Fitch Ratings recently downgraded China's debt, as the nation's credit soared from 125 percent to 200 percent of GDP in only 4 years.[163] Since 2008, China's domestic credit has skyrocketed from $9 trillion to roughly $23 trillion—a truly unprecedented debt explosion. While the US Federal Reserve, the European Central Bank, and other Western governments have been rightly criticized for printing too much money, China makes them look frugal by comparison. Much of China's debt was incurred building empty stadiums, trains, and airports in an effort to keep growth stable during the Great Recession. The result, however, has been to catapult China past the point of diminishing returns. At the beginning of the Great Recession, a dollar of debt created roughly a dollar of growth in China. Today, it takes *four* dollars of debt to create a *single* dollar of growth. [164]

And that means China's runway for future growth is disappearing fast.

China's unwieldy state-run economic system implicitly renders most of its largest firms "too big to fail," creating moral hazards in the near-term and allowing debt to fester over the long-term, making it more difficult for China to successfully transition to a consumer-based, post-industrial economy. Put simply, there are practical limits to economic engineering—and China is testing those limits. [165] [166]

Millennials may confront a very different Peoples' Republic than their parents.

If China's debt bubble bursts, it would certainly dash the country's military ambitions, strengthening US *Military Primacy*. However, a Chinese debt crisis many magnitudes greater than America's recent housing bubble would generate economic shockwaves around the world, seriously damaging US growth and undermining *Economic Dynamism*. Worse, it might produce crippling domestic instability within China. No longer a rising dragon, China might quickly become an economic and political basket case, with nuclear weapons in the mix. The United States would then have an immediate interest in restoring stability to the country.

China's *third challenge* is that its economy is dumb rather than dynamic.

Like Japan and South Korea before it, China transformed its relative poverty into an economic advantage. It used its cheap labor to manufacture cheap products, attracting hefty foreign investment and fueling stupendous economic growth. [167]

But that was the easy part.

China's current economic model only works if its people are poor. And as foreign investment rolls in, wages rise. Costs go up. Goods get more expensive. Exports fall. Then, foreign investment slows and the economy seizes up.

It's China's catch-22: By becoming rich, it risks becoming poor.

In 2008, China staved off recession with massive infusions of government cash. However, without actual consumers for its countless empty stadiums, factories and houses, these "investments" will seriously slow long-term economic growth. Basically, China is using tomorrow's fuel to power today's economic engine. [168]

Difficult though it will be, China has only one halfway decent option: Transition from a dumb economy (one that makes cheap stuff) to a dynamic economy (one that buys cheap stuff), like the United States. Only then can China promote *domestic* demand and maintain economic growth over the long term. This is probably (hopefully) what China will attempt to do.

And that's good for America's *Economic Dynamism*.

How? It will even the playing field, tilt manufacturing back to the United States, and force China to compete in the innovation-economy. Millennials grew up at a time when US manufacturing was losing ground to China, with its seemingly endless supply of cheap labor and cheap products. However, as China seeks to develop a more dynamic economy, it must allow wages to rise so that domestic consumption can rise with it. It's the only way forward. Essentially, people have to make more money so they can spend more money.

As a result, making cheap stuff cannot remain China's special sauce.

When wages and prices rise, other factors—such as quality, consistency, and innovation—become increasingly important. The ability of the Chinese economy to *create*—not just *assemble*—will be tested. By the 2030s, China's top-down, command-and-control economy will have lost its much-ballyhooed manufacturing edge to lower-cost rivals, like Indonesia and Mexico. It will also be forced to defend its manufacturing turf against a resurgent United States, which will enjoy energy independence, shorter supply chains, greater productivity and a more competitive currency. At the same time, China's new consumer-economy will be pitted against modern, knowledge-based economies, with generations of innovation under their belts.

A level playing field isn't China's natural ecosystem.

Unlike the United States, which demonstrated enormous *Economic Dynamism* during its late-19th Century salad days, modern China demonstrates primarily the ability to copy, cheaply. While Chinese ancients invented papermaking, gunpowder, and the compass, their modern descendants lag far behind. China's top-down economic model produces innovations here and there, but it has experienced nowhere near the level of invention the US generated in the early 20th Century, when it was coming of age—and nothing like today's level of American invention. Chinese economists now openly complain that heavy-handed state-run academic and business systems are simply incapable of fostering the type of entrepreneurial dynamism that makes large-scale invention and scientific research possible. [169]

Just consider that *eight* Nobel Prize winners are of Chinese descent, yet *every single one* either was or eventually became a US Citizen.[170] That's a staggering statistic—and one that reveals just how far China must go to defeat the United States in the innovation arena it is preparing to enter.

Sure, it's easy to believe that China's studious youth will eat the lunch of America's lazy, ne'er-do-well Millennials. However, even China's vaunted talent for producing scientists and engineers appears to be little more than a mirage. None of the world's top 20 universities are in China. And although the United States produces roughly 70,000 engineering graduates annually, compared to 600,000 in China, the numbers simply don't hold up under scrutiny. Fully half of China's 600,000 engineering graduates hold Associates degrees, rather than Bachelors degrees. The US only counts 4-year degrees. That's not a knock on Associates degrees, merely an observation that the comparison is distorted at best. More importantly, a McKinsey Global Institute study found that human resource managers in multinational companies considered only 10 percent of Chinese engineers to be employable compared with 81 percent of American graduates. [171]

Not bad for a bunch of lazy Millennials wielding nothing more than their participation trophies.

In the 21st Century, innovation is the name of the game. China knows it and has taken steps to boost its own domestic creative capacity. However, the recent surge in Chinese patent applications appears to be something of an illusion, with many filings spurred by government quotas rather than genuine, you know, *innovation*.

The result: Less than a third of Chinese patent applications were classified as innovation patents, with studies finding that Chinese patents tend to be of lower quality than those produced in other countries. Essentially, the Chinese government decides how many patents it wants and then doles out cash until those targets are met, regardless of merit. [172]

Innovation isn't measured by how much paperwork you fill out, although its easy to see how a statist regime could confuse the latter with the former. Innovation is about changing the world; developing new technologies that affect the marketplace. This type of innovation—let's call it practical innovation—is often measured by Total Factor Productivity or TFP. Prior to 2007, China had been making strides in TFP. But since then, it's been steadily backsliding. [173] *Foreign Policy's* Minxin Pei sums it up: "The region's hierarchical culture, centralized bureaucracy, weak private universities, and emphasis on rote learning and test-taking will continue to hobble its efforts to clone the United States' finest research institutions." [174]

China is no longer functionally communist. However, it is not, as some say, a practitioner of "state-run capitalism." Such a term is oxymoronic. The state cannot *run* capitalism because capitalism, by definition, is not centrally managed. It leaves the lion's hare of decision-making (what to buy, what to pay, what to produce) to the individual. The alternative is simply statism by another name. A more accurate description for the Chinese system would be crony capitalism—the very thing we're struggling to defeat here at home.

Indeed, you might say China is suffering from a very advanced case of crony capitalism, so entangled are the interests of the state and its pseudo-private sector. Whether you call it state-run capitalism or crony capitalism, it's not a philosophy. It is not an exportable economic model or even really an idea—it's the corruption of an idea. It's capitalism gone wrong; it's a haphazard, frat house form of economics based on patronage, rather than the purposed allocation of resources, as in communism or capitalism. Even if China achieves a consumer-based economy by the 2030s, its innovation game will be hamstrung by a reliance on crony capitalism.

And by 2035, it will be a whole new ballgame.

China will face tremendous difficulty competing on a level playing field against seasoned rivals with dynamic economies and cultures that prize individual initiative and creativity. While the US has its own economic problems—including a number of self-inflicted wounds that render it vulnerable—it's next 20 years look to be far more stable than China's. Afflicted by bad cases of *debt, demographics,* and *dumb,* China is unlikely to dethrone the United States as top dog of the international order anytime soon. To prosper, China will be forced to do that which few great nations have done successfully: Shed decades of social, cultural and political programming; abandon central planning; embrace creative destruction.

For America, this idea is natural. For Millennials, it is natural. For China, it is not.

Fountain of Youth

China's demographic crisis threatens its political, social and economic stability.

It's not alone.

In fact, throughout the world, developed nations are not having enough babies. As a result, most advanced economies are on a path to experience traumatic population decline, which will not only strain the resources of governments around the globe but also shrink the available workforce and consumer base.

Essentially, more people *taking,* fewer people *making.*

Fortunately, the United States need not share this fate. When it comes to healthy demographics, America long ago discovered the secret to eternal life: *Immigration.*

Immigration is fuel for the American forge, vital water for its fountain of youth. It is why, among advanced economies, the US population is quite young—second only to India. However, before I write another word, I must draw a distinction between legal and *illegal* immigration. Unlike *illegal* immigration, *legal* immigration is neither an uncomfortable American convenience nor an undue

American burden; it is our lifeblood; it is an American *necessity*. Legal immigration makes healthy, stable population growth possible. Without it, the *Five Pillars of American Power* will crumble.

To the extent that we resemble Rome, it is most evident in this respect: The Romans depended upon military conquest to fill their coffers. The United States does not conquer other nations; it trades with them. As a result, we require a constant flow of immigrants to create new markets, build new companies, and power new industries.

By the mid-21st Century, many advanced economies (and even many developing ones, like China) will be grappling with virtually unmanageable, upside-down-pyramid-style demographics, sapping economic vitality. In this environment, nearly every developed nation on earth will begin aggressively competing for foreign talent. They will need immigration to avoid demographic decline, just as we do.

Healthy population growth and overseas talent-scouting is essential to *Economic Dynamism*. From Pfizer and US Steel to eBay and Google, immigrants or their children founded 40 percent of America's largest companies. A fourth of all high tech companies founded between 1995 and 2005 can claim at least one immigrant founder, while fully three-fourths of the companies funded by US venture capital firms field foreign-born talent in the company's senior leadership.[175]

First generation immigrants start businesses at a rate 27 percent higher than non-immigrants. They're also more likely to be college-educated, with 57 percent holding at least a bachelor's degree, and more likely to earn higher incomes, with 63 percent reaching the top third income bracket.[176]

The importance of legal immigration extends beyond small business startups. In the coming decades, most major industrialized countries will face STEM (Science, Technology, Engineering, Mathematics) degree shortfalls—and the US is no exception. By 2018, there will be an estimated 2.8 million job openings in STEM fields and, like China, Japan and Europe, we're not on track to produce enough skilled domestic workers to fill those posts.

In order to fill those slots, Millennial leaders will revise national immigration policy.

The first thing to change will be the outmoded, factory-style system of work visas. It's antiquated and counterproductive. For example, in 2013, 40,000 highly skilled workers seeking a temporary work visa in the United States received notice that their H-1B petition would not even be reviewed because 125,000 applications had been received for 85,000 slots. These workers are among the most highly educated, highly skilled in their fields. And we told them to stay home.[177]

In keeping with Millennials' special affinity for entrepreneurship, the second thing to change will be our policy toward foreign-born small business startups. Right now, a foreign national with an idea like Facebook or eBay would have a tough time sprouting their company in the US because visas for entrepreneurs typically require an upfront investment of $1 million with the promise of 10 full-time jobs over a two-year period.

That's outdated, Industrial Age nonsense. Many of today's most promising new businesses are professional service firms, software manufacturers, dot-com companies and the like. They often begin as garage-entrepreneurs, with the most promising young startups of the Information Age seldom sporting million-dollar initial investments or large workforces at the outset. However, one day, some of these firms grow up into Facebook, Google or PayPal and spin off jobs and wealth for thousands.[178]

As a matter of principle, I do not advocate amnesty or illegal immigration. These practices run counter to the Rule of Law, which is essential to *Domestic Stability.* I also recognize that these hot-button subjects—so intensely controversial in 2014—will be viewed in an entirely different context by 2035. Two decades from now, the problem will not be scarcity of jobs. The problem will be scarcity of people. As a result, we will no longer be arguing about how to keep people out. We will be arguing about how to lure them in.

As Millennials rise, America's horse-and-buggy-era immigration system will face bipartisan pressure to reform. Before the 2020s are out, an Information Age overhaul of immigration policy will recognize the fluidity of capital—including talent—and allow US firms to hire and retain skilled foreign workers. It will also revamp the clunky, Industrial Age immigration bureaucracy that currently chases away foreign-born entrepreneurs and fends off highly skilled specialists. By 2035, if we aren't outright stapling green cards to diplomas, we'll come pretty damn close.

The global talent race is right around the corner. And the money, markets, and world-class post-secondary education system needed to win it are already here, in the United States. Our free enterprise system remains vibrant, even if it is constantly harassed by an administration that neither understands nor values it. Our markets are vast and our venture capital system, unmatched. The best and the brightest, the most talented in the world, want to come to America.

Our economic rivals are not content to leave it this way. They want to reverse their own brain drains. They want their talent back; they want their kids to come home—not become Americans. In the coming years, the demographic crises in these countries will make them more aggressive competitors for top talent.

One thing is clear: If we do not win the coming talent race, someone else will. And we may one day wake up to find throngs of American students venturing abroad to study in India, China, or Brazil—and then seeking their dreams and their fortunes in the countries that educated them.

Manufacturing Renaissance

We're going to start making things again.

As the late 2020s spark efforts to halt demographic decline and maintain *Domestic Stability* and *Economic Dynamism*, the US will be well on its way to strengthening another *Pillar of American Power*: *Energy Security*. Indeed, by 2035, the United States will finally achieve energy independence.[179]

Since 2006, American oil production has risen by more than 50 percent—faster than anywhere else on the planet. At the same time, natural gas production has climbed more than 30 percent, making the United States the world's leading producer of natural gas. Within two decades, it is altogether possible that the US will not only be the planet's top producer of oil, coal, and natural gas but also, for the first time in generations, completely *energy secure.* [180]

This will prove to be an economic miracle-maker.

Once upon a time, China enjoyed a 25 to 30 percent cost advantage over the United States. New research indicates that— thanks in part to our domestic energy boom—China's advantage has already slipped to a mere 4 percent and will disappear completely by 2020. This is causing some manufacturers to seek new labor markets, while others have re-shored to the United States, where cheaper domestic energy, greater intellectual property protection, shorter supply chains, and the higher productivity of American workers is sufficient to offset costs.[181] [182]

In fact, upon factoring in labor and energy costs, productivity growth and exchange rates, the United States quickly emerges as one of the most competitive manufacturing economies in the world. This recent development, brought about over the last decade, is a product of regular productivity improvements and robust domestic energy resources, among other things. China, on the other hand, is losing ground—partly because of wage hikes, rising energy costs, and declining productivity growth—and partly because other low-cost competitors, such as Indonesia, India, and Mexico, are moving onto their turf. [183]

Millennials grew up in an era of domestic manufacturing decline. But they will come of age at a time of manufacturing rebirth. By the 2030s, American factories—once thought destined for extinction— will rise like a phoenix, humming along on cheap, abundant domestic energy. This, along with rising wages in the developing world, will fundamentally alter the cost equation for American companies and encourage the return of good-paying manufacturing jobs.

2035

When 2035 rolls around, the world will look different—but not necessarily worse.

In fact, it may look a good deal better. By the time Millennials are leading America's public institutions and top corporations, expectations will have realigned. Few will remember the Industrial Age economy that Boomers inherited. Corporations will be leaner. Small business will proliferate. Independent contractors will abound. Unions will be smaller and weaker. Even government will begin to slim down, simplify, decentralize, and increasingly outsource to private-sector vendors.

By this time, if China has successfully avoided a debt-induced economic meltdown and managed to transition to a consumer-economy, its exports will be much more expensive. A lot of manufacturing will return to the United States, boosting prospects for middle-aged Millennials and increasing demand for skilled labor. That will necessitate a small resurgence of vocational education, which will strengthen the Middle Class. At the same time, America's oil and gas boom will foster energy independence. The world will be flatter, smaller. Competition will be intense. But it will be based on ideas, innovation, and talent.

And America remains a magnet for all three.

I predict that 2035 will find *the Five Pillars of American Power— Economic Dynamism, Cultural Universality, Domestic Stability, Energy Security* and *Military Primacy*—in reasonably good stead.

Thanks to its world-class universities and vast consumer economy, America's *Economic Dynamism* will benefit from strong immigration, which will allow the United States to avoid the demographic poison now seeping into Russia, China, Japan, and Europe. It will also benefit from the rise of America's Millennials—a thrifty, choice-driven, and entrepreneurial generation that has already learned to expect less from the social safety net devised by its predecessor generations.

At the same time, *Energy Security* will become a reality for the first time in generations, as America's strong portfolio of traditional energy helps facilitate a minor manufacturing renaissance and fosters a more diverse domestic economy.

For the first time in modern history, America will face genuine cultural competition, thanks to the spread and saturation of personal technology. Other countries will make increasingly significant contributions to popular culture. However, America's *Cultural Universality* will endure. After all, our core value—*choice*—is not only the watchword of the 21st Century; it is the value nearest to the human heart. Technology, namely the Internet, will multiply the delivery systems for American culture and erode the iron-fisted control of statist regimes that attempt to resist.

Military Primacy is the *Pillar of American Power* that we've discussed least. There can be little doubt that, barring a meltdown, China's fast-growing economy will enable it to make ever-larger investments in national defense. With their somewhat libertarian attitudes toward foreign policy, Millennials may not have an appetite for the defense spending required to deter China. That is a serious problem—and one that may precipitate conflict in the Pacific.

However, China's problems may be even greater. While the PRC's internal security budget is a secret, many analysts believe the Chinese Communist Party spends *more* money defending itself from its own people—in the form of Internet censorship and internal security forces—than it spends defending the country from foreign powers. This two-sided conflict is more than a threat to China's long-term stability. It represents a very real, very tangible drain on China's national defense budget.[184]

And it isn't China's only big geopolitical problem. China is fenced in by hostile terrain and surrounded by rivals, such as Japan and India, as well as a host of smaller countries—such as South Korea, the Philippines, Singapore, and Taiwan—which fear China's rise and have sought to strengthen ties with the United States.

Finally, *Domestic Stability* will be shaken by the fragmentation and reorganization of several major American institutions, such as the news media. Moreover, government's awkward, sluggish transition to the Information Age—which will include acrimonious battles over entitlement reform—may lead to social unrest. Nonetheless, this unrest will be temporary. After two decades of internal strife, the United States will emerge with a more modern federal government, fewer unions, and more sustainable entitlement programs. Its demographics will be healthy and its institutions smaller, though far more credible.

Empowered by technology, Millennials are molding a modern meritocracy—one that celebrates entrepreneurship, individual initiative and creative thinking. It's a model that ties an individual's success to her talents and determination, not her seniority. It's a world without guarantees. But it's not a bad world. It avoids the pitfalls of unrealistic expectations fostered by unsustainable promises. It promotes possibilities rather than liabilities, opportunities rather than entitlements. It positions the United States to thrive in a highly competitive global marketplace, where our safe, stable and relatively free society is not nearly as unique as it once was; where our best selling points are our full-throated endorsement of creative destruction and our passion for individualism, risk-taking and idea-making.

Aided by these mighty tailwinds, a new American Phoenix is poised to rise from the ashes of the old order—confident, prosperous and free.

CHAPTER 10
CONCLUSION

Things will get harder before they get easier.

A toxic combination of defense cuts, amateur foreign policy, piss-poor economics, overregulation, and dangerous levels of debt have weakened our country. *Debt*, in particular, has diminished American prosperity, limited our foreign policy options, and rendered the United States vulnerable to a rising China.

We're broke. But we're not yet broken.

America's cultural *hardware* remains the best in the world. Our economy boasts the finest combination of breadth, depth, size, diversity and innovation. The *Five Pillars of American Power*, which serve as the basis for America's global leadership, remain unmatched, but not unchallenged. Increasingly, the United States will face tests of its economic, military, and cultural dominance. With new powers rising, America must learn how to manage a wider chorus of voices—both allies and rivals.

In this time of turmoil, a new generation is also rising.

Born in the 1980s and 90s, Millennials were shaped by *three forces*: The *tech-effect*—an impatient, choice-driven ethos inspired by abundant access to personal technology; the *Great Recession*, which produced economic setbacks not seen since before the Second World War; and the wide array of *unmet expectations* brought about by those setbacks.

It's commonly believed that Millennials are too soft, too spoiled, and too selfish.

The most widely cited culprit is the notorious *participation trophy*—symbol of everything wrong with this generation of lazy, narcissistic, incompetents. Well, as a card-carrying Millennial, I can report that I've accumulated my fair share of participation trophies over the years—typically for something sports-related. I can't remember scoring a single goal in eight years of playing soccer. Seriously, *eight years*. However, I'm reasonably certain that trophies were doled out regardless, and usually with some pomp and circumstance. We all had trophies. But that never stopped us from figuring out who the best players were. And it never deluded me into thinking I was anything but lousy at soccer. In that sense, the trophies became meaningless bobbles, easily gained and quickly forgotten.

Put another way, I might have thought myself a good soccer player if the only element to the game was the ritual of collecting participation trophies. But every week, the temptation to believe I was any good at the game collided with the reality that I wasn't very good at all—particularly when I saw better players score goals and steal balls while I dragged myself aimlessly up and down the field.

A note: To those thinking about getting rid of scorekeepers at little league soccer games—that's just crazy talk. Scorekeeping makes us better. The world keeps score. Your kid will figure that out one way or another. You probably spent a lot of time going through baby name books and buying organic food so that junior will have the best chance at getting ahead in life. But he won't get very far if he's the last one to figure out that winning matters. So climb down from your sanctimonious perch and take a moment to reflect on all the times adversity made you stronger, smarter, better at whatever it is you do—unless all you do is try to get rid of scorekeepers at kids' soccer games. In which case, you should probably just go home and admire your own wall of participation trophies. *Embarrassing.*

Ostensibly, our parents invented the much-ballyhooed participation trophy for our benefit. But these shiny trinkets were really designed to make mom and dad happy. Most of us figured that out, eventually. That's why I don't put much stock in participation trophies. If those silly paperweights gave us anything, it was a thirst for the genuine article, the real deal; a desire to go get an *authentic* trophy—one that we earned. That's why Millennials regard the entrepreneur more highly than any other figure. It's why studies show we want to start small businesses, be good parents, and achieve economic success more than any other generation. We've figured out the difference between a participation trophy and a real one. And we want the real deal.

In the coming decades, my theories will be tested. *Millennials* will be tested.

Complex problems lay ahead: A looming debt crisis, a rising

China, demographic decline, institutional decay, and fierce economic competition. No participation trophies will be awarded. The prize for second place: To preside over the decline of a great nation—to witness the demise of mankind's finest idea.

But I don't think collapse is the cards.

Millennials will lead a *Great Transition* that will change media, government and the American economy. This transition will be motivated by *three forces*: First, Millennials' tech-effect will fragment traditional media outlets, paving the way to a more robust conservative voice in entertainment, education and the news media. Second, Millennials will drag government from the Industrial Age to the Information Age. Their choice-driven, fix-it-now, trust-the-individual, keep-it-local mentality will have a positive impact on Washington's aging institutions. Third, Millennials will finally overcome the Recession-induced economic stagnation that delayed so many life decisions, from family formation and marriage to long-simmering startup dreams. In the post-Obama years, pent-up entrepreneurial energy will power a wave of new small businesses and strengthen long-term economic growth.

Politically, Millennials are likely to become something of a tossup generation. Expect early-wave Millennials, recalling the Bush years, to remain reasonably liberal. At the same time, look for late-wave Millennials, disillusioned with the Obama years, to chart a path to the right. This generation's aversion to rigid political categories suggests that the coming politics will be less ideological and more volatile. Don't be surprised by the widespread appearance of non-traditional political orientations, such as "Pro-Life Economic Liberals" and "Pro-Same-Sex-Marriage Fiscal Conservatives." Overall, however, barring a calamitous Republican presidency, look for fiscal conservatism to rise over the next two decades.

In fact, just look at the status quo—it's already beginning to happen. Since taking office in 2009, Barack Obama has presided over a steady decline in liberalism among the voting public. A cross-survey index of public opinion data indicates the country is now *more* conservative than when it re-elected Ronald Reagan in 1984. This data is not based on voters' self-descriptions of their own ideologies; meaning, it does not matter how liberal or conservative voters *think* they are. Instead, it is based on the public's views on *specific issues*—a far better measure in this case. The rise of conservatism has little to do with the success of the Republican Party. Instead, it is the mark of a struggling presidency, which is quickly converting disciples into doubters.[185]

With Millennials' choice-based philosophy standing in for deep-seated political ideology, look for the notion of *personal freedom* to seep into every aspect of our culture, from fiscal and social policy, to the media, to business and consumer behavior. On balance, that's good. After all, the notion of *choice* is essential to the American experience. Reviving this notion and putting it on something of a pedestal may very well produce a libertarian-tinged conservative renaissance, realigning our politics, and, ultimately, strengthening the *Five Pillars of American Power.*

You may believe me, or you may think I'm nuts. While you decide, let me make a recommendation: Find your favorite Frenchman—or *Frenchwoman*, if you must.

Since most of them are communists and quitters (a joke, sort of), your choices are limited. So, I pick America's first foreign biographer, Alexis de Tocqueville. If you've heard of him but don't know why, fear not. Alexis is best known for *Democracy in America,* a compelling two-volume work based on his travels stateside.

Tocqueville once wondered if a democratic people—if a true Republic—could weather a great storm, a national calamity. "It is difficult to say what degree of effort a democratic government may be capable of making on the occurrence of a national crisis," wrote Tocqueville, in a very 19th Century-sounding way. "No great democratic republic has hitherto existed in the world [...] The United States affords the first example of the kind."

When Tocqueville wrote *Democracy in America*, the United States had existed for a mere half-century. In its War for Independence, "extraordinary efforts were made with enthusiasm for the service of the country," according to Tocqueville. "But as the contest was prolonged private selfishness began to reappear. No money was brought into the public treasury; few recruits could be raised for the army; the people still wished to acquire independence, but would not employ the only means by which it could be obtained."

We lionize America's founding—*as we should.* We often forget, however, that our Founders faced the very same selfishness and shortsightedness that we face today. Imagine: Our young Republic, struggling to shuffle off the coil of foreign tyranny, *nearly failing to field an army* because of flagging patriotism. To say they stuck with it in the face of adversity would be an understatement.

So, we face bloated entitlements? *They faced death.*

We face overregulation? They faced death.

We face high taxes? They faced death.

If they didn't surrender in the face of death, what right do we have to give up in the face of problems we can solve? Tocqueville wondered if, when it really came down to it, Americans would fight to preserve their freedoms.

I know what my grandparents' generation would say to that. I know what every generation of Americans all the way back to that founding generation would say.

What will we say?

Will we toss in the towel because the Man in the Oval doesn't get it?

Will we give up because our neighbor doesn't get it?

Will we quit the field because the media doesn't get it?

In those early days, when our newborn Republic teetered on the brink of collapse, I bet our Founders had many dark nights of the soul. I bet they had countless reasons to give up, to go home, to toss in the towel. But they didn't. And they won.

I think we'll win, too.

I think we'll fight harder because we have a lot to lose. Together, Americans slew the sin of slavery, vanquished the forces of fascism, overpowered evil empires, and lit the torch of freedom for the whole world to see. We have overcome droughts, fires, hurricanes, and even super storms. We put a man on the moon, split the atom, wired the world, launched our handiwork beyond the reaches of the solar system, peered into the moment of creation and scrutinized the subatomic particles that knit the universe together. We have freed whole continents, inaugurated new epochs, launched countless new industries, established a new international order, and outlasted economic depressions and recessions time and time again. We are equal to the task—any task—today, tomorrow and forever.

And Barack Obama? We'll outlast him, too.

History does not judge us by our immunity to mistakes. It judges us by our capacity for rectifying them. Tocqueville figured that out nearly two centuries ago when he wrote, "The great privilege of the Americans does not consist in being more enlightened than other nations, but in being able to repair the faults they may commit."

The botched rollout and broken promises of Obamacare are unraveling Barack Obama's presidency. Liberalism is undoing itself. Americans are learning their true interests, by experience—the best teacher around.

And fortunately, in the United States, the impact of our politicians need not last forever. "The authority which public men possess in America is so brief and they are so soon commingled with the ever changing population of the country that the acts of a community frequently leave fewer traces than events in a private family," explained Tocqueville.

History teaches us that our modern challenges are neither

insurmountable nor entirely unique. Americans can, as Alexis de Tocqueville suggested 17 decades ago, learn "their true interests," regain "the right path," and repair their mistakes.

Indeed, that we Americans are so quick to criticize ourselves; that we are so apt to notice our own faults; that we are so concerned with the views of others, so ready to accept the possibility of our own demise, is one of the better safeguards against it. Though Americans are sometimes ridiculed as hardheaded or narrow-minded, few superpowers have had a conscience to match their strength.

We're different.

It is true that, throughout human history, many great nations have survived struggle and hardship, only to succumb to prosperity and plenty. But the American people are more dynamic than any to precede them; better fitted for greatness than any before us. Ours is a nation devised by man's mind, not merely dictated by his geography; forged by struggle, fired by imagination, fated to lead.

Conceived by the wise, this nation may long endure the administration of fools.

You can doubt my conclusions. You can think I'm off my rocker. You're free to remain a pessimist. You're even free to quit the fight. But even the toughest pessimist and the surliest curmudgeon must acknowledge that our odds of reviving this country are still better than the odds those poor bastards in tri-cornered hats faced building it. And you know, I don't think they sacrificed *their* lives, *their* liberty and *their* pursuit of happiness so that *we would have the right to quit on ourselves.*

ABOUT THE AUTHOR

Head of the national free market watchdog group, Free Market America, Ryan Houck is the writer, producer and voice of numerous hit videos, including the overnight YouTube phenomenon, If I Wanted America to Fail—which earned more than 2.7 million views on YouTube alone, headlined The Drudge Report and captivated conservative media circles during the Earth Day news cycle.

Called the radical environmentalist's "worst nightmare" by Bill Frezza of the Competitive Enterprise Institute, Houck's previous work includes numerous published journal and newspaper articles as well as documentary directing credits. Houck's background includes leading successful multi-million dollar campaigns against radical environmental interests in Florida and across the country.

END NOTES

[1] Joffe, Josef, *The American Interest,* November / December 2013

[2] Joffe, Josef, *The American Interest,* November / December 2013

[3] Fein, Esther B., *The New York Times,* November 28, 1989.
(**http://www.nytimes.com/1989/11/28/world/clamor-in-the-east-unshackled-czech-workers-declare-their-independence.html?src=pm**)

[4] Fein, Esther B., *The New York Times,* November 28, 1989.
(**http://www.nytimes.com/1989/11/28/world/clamor-in-the-east-unshackled-czech-workers-declare-their-independence.html?src=pm**)

[5] Jefferson, Thomas "To Henry Lee - Thomas Jefferson The Works, vol. 12 (Correspondence and Papers 1816 – 1826; 1905". The Online Library of Liberty. May 8, 1825.)

[6] Forbes, Steve, *Forbes,* October 30, 2013
(**http://www.forbes.com/sites/othercomments/2013/10/30/u-s-national-debt-1-1-million-per-taxpayer/**)

[7] Boccia, Romina, Acosta Fraser, Alison, and Goff, Emily, *The Heritage Foundation,* Accessed online on Nov. 4, 2013
(**http://www.heritage.org/research/reports/2013/08/federal-spending-by-the-numbers-2013**)

[8] Bureau of the Public Debt

[9] Schroeder, Robert, *MarketWatch,* September 17, 2013

(http://www.marketwatch.com/story/cbo-issues-fresh-long-term-debt-warning-2013-09-17?link=MW_pulse)

[10] DeSilver, Drew, *Pew Research*, October 9, 2013 9
(http://www.pewresearch.org/fact-tank/2013/10/09/5-facts-about-the-national-debt-what-you-should-know/)

[11] Monan, Zhang, *Project-Syndicate*, January 8, 2014
(http://www.project-syndicate.org/commentary/zhang-monan-explains-why-china-is-experiencing-a-worsening-credit-crunch-despite-a-buildup-of-leverage-in-china-since-2008)

[12] DeSilver, Drew, *Pew Research*, October 9, 2013 9
(http://www.pewresearch.org/fact-tank/2013/10/09/5-facts-about-the-national-debt-what-you-should-know/)

[13] Conerly, Bill, *Forbes*, October 25, 2013
(http://www.forbes.com/sites/billconerly/2013/10/25/future-of-the-dollar-as-world-reserve-currency/2/)

[14] The International Monetary Fund, 2013.

[15] Starrs, Sean, *Politico*, February 24, 2014
(http://www.politico.com/magazine/story/2014/02/america-didnt-decline-it-went-global-103865_Page2.html#.U-UenIBdUs4)

[16] Bloomberg Rankings, *Bloomberg*, February 1, 2013
(http://www.bloomberg.com/slideshow/2013-02-01/50-most-innovative-countries.html#slide51)

[17] *RealClearScience*, Top 10 Counties with Greatest Scientific Impact
(*http://www.realclearscience.com/lists/top_10_countries_with_greatest_scientific_impact/h-index.html?state=stop*)

[18] The Small Business Administration, 2012

[19] The Guardian, DataBlog
(http://www.theguardian.com/news/datablog/2012/mar/15/top-100-universities-times-higher-education)

[20] Fisher, Max, *The Washington Post*, January 13, 2014
(http://www.washingtonpost.com/blogs/worldviews/wp/2014/01/13/40-more-maps-that-explain-the-world/)

[21] Encyclopedia Britannica, May 9, 2014

(http://www.britannica.com/EBchecked/topic/616563/United-States/78003/Religious-groups#toc78005)

[22] The CIA World Factbook, 2012

[23] Pew Research, July 12, 2012

[24] Serwer, Andy, *Fortune,* September 5, 2013
(http://money.cnn.com/2013/09/05/news/economy/energy-boom.pr.fortune/index.html)

[25] Domm, Patti, *CNBC*, March 2, 2013
(http://www.cnbc.com/id/100513916)

[26] Suderman, Peter, *Reason*, February 26, 2014
(http://reason.com/blog/2014/02/26/the-us-military-budget-is-bigger-than-th)

[27] Zakaria, Fareed, *The Washington Post,* May 29, 2013
(http://www.washingtonpost.com/opinions/fareed-zakaria-obamas-disciplined-leadership-is-right-for-today/2014/05/29/7b4eb460-e76d-11e3-afc6-a1dd9407abcf_story.html)

[28] Joffe, Josef, *The American Interest,* November / December 2013

[29] Beach, Chris and Howard, Alison, *The National Review,* January 13, 2014
(http://www.nationalreview.com/article/368236/millennials-are-tiring-liberal-failures-chris-beach-alison-howard)

[30] Mason, John, *Forbes,* August 12, 2013

[31] Kotkin, Joel, *Forbes,* April 21, 2014
(http://www.forbes.com/sites/joelkotkin/2014/04/21/turn-of-the-screwed-does-the-gop-have-a-shot-at-wooing-millennials/)

[32] Pew Research Center, February, 2010
(http://www.pewsocialtrends.org/files/2010/10/millennials-confident-connected-open-to-change.pdf)

[33] Pew Research Center, February, 2010
(http://www.pewsocialtrends.org/files/2010/10/millennials-confident-connected-open-to-change.pdf)

[34] Adams, Susan, *Forbes,* August, 23, 2012

[35] Glassman, Mark, *The Washington Post,* August 30, 2013 (**http://www.washingtonpost.com/opinions/five-myths-about-millennials/2013/08/30/a6d9a854-ff6c-11e2-9711-3708310f6f4d_story.html**)

[36] Ellis, Blake, *Fortune,* May 17, 2013 (**http://money.cnn.com/2013/05/17/pf/college/student-debt/index.html**)

[37] Williams, Chris, *The Guardian,* August 27, 2013 (**http://www.theguardian.com/commentisfree/2013/aug/27/student-loan-debt-cripple-young-americans**)

[38] Pew Social Trends, August 1, 2013 (**http://www.pewsocialtrends.org/2013/08/01/a-rising-share-of-young-adults-live-in-their-parents-home/**)

[39] Winograd, Morley and Hais, Michael D., *New Geography,* July 27, 2008 (**http://www.newgeography.com/content/00119-a-return-avalon**)

[40] Winograd, Morley and Hais, Michael D., *New Geography,* July 27, 2008 (**http://www.newgeography.com/content/00119-a-return-avalon**)

[41] Winograd, Morley and Hais, Michael D., *New Geography,* July 27, 2008 (**http://www.newgeography.com/content/00119-a-return-avalon**)

[42] Kotkin, Joel, *The Daily Beast,* November 10, 2013

[43] Winograd, Morley and Hais, Michael D., *New Geography,* July 27, 2008 (**http://www.newgeography.com/content/00119-a-return-avalon**)

[44] *Pew Research,* March 7, 2014 (**http://www.pewsocialtrends.org/2014/03/07/millennials-in-adulthood/4/**)

[45] Smith, Kyle, *The New York Post,* July 19, 2014 (**http://nypost.com/2014/07/19/could-young-people-be-the-next-generation-of-republicans/**)

[46] Klein, Ezra, *The Washington Post,* May 9, 2013 citing a survey by the *Pew Research Center.*

(http://www.washingtonpost.com/blogs/wonkblog/wp/2013/05
/09/joel-stein-is-wrong-about-millennials-in-one-chart/

[47] *Wait But Why,* Accessed Oct 20, 2013
(http://www.waitbutwhy.com/2013/09/why-generation-y-
yuppies-are-unhappy.html)

[48] Edsall, Thomas B., *The New York Times,* July 15, 2014
(http://www.nytimes.com/2014/07/16/opinion/thomas-edsall-
a-shift-in-young-democrats-values.html?ref=opinion&_r=0)

[49] Edsall, Thomas B., *The New York Times,* July 15, 2014
(http://www.nytimes.com/2014/07/16/opinion/thomas-edsall-
a-shift-in-young-democrats-values.html?ref=opinion&_r=0)

[50] Edsall, Thomas B., *The New York Times,* July 15, 2014
(http://www.nytimes.com/2014/07/16/opinion/thomas-edsall-
a-shift-in-young-democrats-values.html?ref=opinion&_r=0)

[51] Edsall, Thomas B., *The New York Times,* July 15, 2014
(http://www.nytimes.com/2014/07/16/opinion/thomas-edsall-
a-shift-in-young-democrats-values.html?ref=opinion&_r=0)

[52] Kotkin, Joel, *The Daily Beast,* November 10, 2013

[53] Randall, Eric, *The Boston Daily*, November 4, 2013
(http://www.bostonmagazine.com/news/blog/2013/11/04/bost
on-globe-columnist-pens-lazy-take-lazy-millenials/)

[54] Hartman, Mitchell, *The New York Times,* March 28, 2014
(http://articles.economictimes.indiatimes.com/2014-03-
28/news/48662648_1_work-ethic-young-workers-millennials)

[55] Brownstein, Ronald, *National Journal,* September 19, 2013
(http://www.nationaljournal.com/magazine/the-american-
dream-under-threat-20130919)

[56] Malcom, Hadley, *CNBC,* May 13, 2013
(http://www.cnbc.com/id/100732021)

[57] Solomon, Jesse, *CNN,* February 6, 2014
(http://money.cnn.com/2014/02/06/investing/millennial-
investing/index.html)

[58] De Groote, Michael, *Deseret News*, December 1, 2013

(http://www.deseretnews.com/article/865591508/Frugal-millennials-leading-way-in-hunting-for-bargains-this-holiday-season.html?pg=all)

59 De Groote, Michael, *Deseret News*, December 1, 2013
(http://www.deseretnews.com/article/865591508/Frugal-millennials-leading-way-in-hunting-for-bargains-this-holiday-season.html?pg=all)

60 Hartwell, Sharalyn, *The Examiner*, July 31, 2011
(http://www.examiner.com/article/millennials-most-likely-to-start-their-own-business)

61 Malcom, Hadley, *CNBC*, May 13, 2013
(http://www.cnbc.com/id/100732021)
62 Curtis, Lisa, *Forbes*, November 18, 2013
(http://www.forbes.com/sites/85broads/2013/11/18/the-millennial-startup-revolution/)

63 Swart, Gary, *Forbes*, October 11, 2012
(http://www.forbes.com/sites/jjcolao/2012/10/11/welcome-to-the-new-millennial-economy-goodbye-ownership-hello-access/)

64 Schramm, Carl, *The Kaufman Foundation*, November 10, 2011
(http://www.kauffman.org/newsroom/2012/11/an-entrepreneurial-generation-of-18-to-34yearolds-wants-to-start-companies-when-economy-rebounds-according-to-new-poll)

65 Pinkser, Beth, *Daily Finance*, August 4th, 2013

66 Will, George, *The Washington Post*, February 18, 2014
(http://www.washingtonpost.com/opinions/george-f-will-breaking-the-grip-of-the-unions/2014/02/18/39beb794-98d4-11e3-b88d-f36c07223d88_story.html)

67 Gordon, Jason Steele, *Commentary Magazine*, February 16, 2014
(http://www.commentarymagazine.com/2014/02/16/the-uaws-waterloo/)

68 Will, George, *The Washington Post*, February 18, 2014
(http://www.washingtonpost.com/opinions/george-f-will-breaking-the-grip-of-the-unions/2014/02/18/39beb794-98d4-11e3-b88d-f36c07223d88_story.html)

69 Gordon, Jason Steele, *Commentary Magazine*, February 16, 2014

(http://www.commentarymagazine.com/2014/02/16/the-uaws-waterloo/)

[70] Friedman, Thomas, *The New York Times,* April 30, 2013
(http://www.nytimes.com/2013/05/01/opinion/friedman-its-a-401k-world.html?_r=2&)

[71] Karabell, Zachary, *Reuters,* July 26, 2013
(http://blogs.reuters.com/edgy-optimist/2013/07/26/a-new-american-dream-for-a-new-american-century/)

[72] Friedman, Thomas, *The New York Times,* April 30, 2013
(http://www.nytimes.com/2013/05/01/opinion/friedman-its-a-401k-world.html?_r=2&)

[73] Taylor, Kate, *Entrepreneur,* March 10, 2014
(http://www.entrepreneur.com/article/232062)

[74] Taylor, Kate, *Entrepreneur,* March 10, 2014
(http://www.entrepreneur.com/article/232062)

[75] Taylor, Kate, *Entrepreneur,* March 10, 2014
(http://www.entrepreneur.com/article/232062)

[76] Pew Research Center, February, 2010
(http://www.pewsocialtrends.org/files/2010/10/millennials-confident-connected-open-to-change.pdf)

[77] Priceline.com

[78] Monasco, Britton, *Corante,* September 9, 2004
(http://customer.corante.com/archives/2004/09/09/the_fragmentation_of_fashion.php)

[79] Rasmussen, Scott, *RealClearPolitics,* September 2, 2013
(http://www.realclearpolitics.com/articles/2013/09/02/reality_catching_up_to_the_political_class_119798.html)

[80] Thompson, Clive, *MotherJones,* October, 2013
(http://www.motherjones.com/politics/2013/08/mesh-internet-privacy-nsa-isp)

[81] Carney, Tim, *The Washington Examiner,* August 20, 2013
(http://washingtonexaminer.com/doing-things-together-doesnt-mean-a-big-government-program/article/2534503)

[82] Carney, Tim, *The Washington Examiner,* August 20, 2013 (**http://washingtonexaminer.com/doing-things-together-doesnt-mean-a-big-government-program/article/2534503**)

[83] Hargreaves, Steve, *CNN,* November 7, 2013 (**http://money.cnn.com/2013/11/07/news/economy/highest-paid/index.html**)

[84] Castellanos, Alex, *The Crimson,* May 30, 2013 (**http://www.thecrimson.com/article/2013/5/30/new-world-success/?page=single**)

[85] Friedman, Thomas, *The New York Times*, June 18, 2013 (**http://www.nytimes.com/2013/06/19/opinion/friedman-postcard-from-turkey.html?_r=1&**)

[86] Huston, Warner Todd, *Breitbart,* March 19, 2014 (**http://www.breitbart.com/Big-Government/2014/03/19/Millennials-Don-t-like-Gov-t-Any-More**)

[87] Herbert Stein (1997-05-16). "Herb Stein's Unfamiliar Quotations". Slate magazine. Retrieved February 26, 2014. (**http://www.slate.com/articles/business/it_seems_to_me/1997/05/herb_steins_unfamiliar_quotations.single.html**)

[88] Wehner, Peter, *Commentary*, September 12, 2013 (**http://www.commentarymagazine.com/2013/09/12/the-collapse-of-the-obama-presidency/**)

[89] Krayewski, Ed, *Reason.com*, November 19, 2012 (**http://reason.com/blog/2012/11/19/barack-obama-first-president-re-elected**)

[90] Rayne, Sierra, *The American Thinker*, August 12, 2013 (**http://www.americanthinker.com/2013/08/reagan_vs_obama_it s_not_even_close.html**)

[91] U.S. Election Atlas, Accessed Nov. 15, 2013 (**http://uselectionatlas.org/RESULTS/**)

[92] Fournier, Ron, *The National Journal*, December 4, 2013 (**http://www.nationaljournal.com/politics/millennials-abandon-obama-and-obamacare-20131204**)

[93] Quinnipiac University National Poll, November 12, 2013

(http://www.quinnipiac.edu/institutes-and-centers/polling-institute/search-releases/search-results/release-detail?ReleaseID=1975&What=&strArea=;&strTime=3)

[94] Quinnipiac University National Poll, November 12, 2013
(http://www.quinnipiac.edu/institutes-and-centers/polling-institute/search-releases/search-results/release-detail?ReleaseID=1975&What=&strArea=;&strTime=3)

[95] Quinnipiac University National Poll, November 12, 2013
(http://www.quinnipiac.edu/institutes-and-centers/polling-institute/search-releases/search-results/release-detail?ReleaseID=1975&What=&strArea=;&strTime=3)

[96] Langer, Gary, *ABC News*, November 19, 2013
(http://abcnews.go.com/blogs/politics/2013/11/botched-aca-rollout-hammers-obama-job-disapproval-reaches-a-career-high/)

[97] Wehner, Peter, *Commentary Magazine,* December 5, 2013
(http://www.commentarymagazine.com/2013/12/05/obamas-coalition-of-the-ascendant-is-collapsing/)

[98] CNN | ORC International Poll, May 29 – June 1, 2014
(http://i2.cdn.turner.com/cnn/2014/images/06/03/cnn.poll.obama.va.pdf)

[99] Fournier, Ron, *the Atlantic,* August 26, 2013
(http://www.theatlantic.com/politics/archive/2013/08/the-outsiders-how-can-millennials-change-washington-if-they-hate-it/278920/)

[100] Pew Research Center for People & Press, November 26, 2013
(http://www.people-press.org/2012/11/26/young-voters-supported-obama-less-but-may-have-mattered-more/)

[101] Tragone, Adam, Young America's Foundation, May 8, 2013
(http://www.yaf.org/adam-tragone-surprise-young-americans-do-not-want-more-government.aspx)

[102] Fournier, Ron, *the Atlantic,* August 26, 2013
(http://www.theatlantic.com/politics/archive/2013/08/the-outsiders-how-can-millennials-change-washington-if-they-hate-it/278920/)

[103] Fournier, Ron, *the Atlantic,* August 26, 2013

(http://www.theatlantic.com/politics/archive/2013/08/the-outsiders-how-can-millennials-change-washington-if-they-hate-it/278920/)

[104] Barone, Michael, *The Washington Examiner,* May 3, 2014
(http://washingtonexaminer.com/younger-millennials-strikingly-more-republican-than-their-millennial-elders/article/2548022)

[105] Jones, Jeffrey M., *Gallup,* January 8, 2014
(http://www.gallup.com/poll/166763/record-high-americans-identify-independents.aspx)

[106] Irvine, Martha, *Associated Press,* October 27, 2012
(http://bigstory.ap.org/article/young-millennials-fiscal-conservatives)

[107] Irvine, Martha, *Associated Press,* October 27, 2012
(http://bigstory.ap.org/article/young-millennials-fiscal-conservatives)

[108] Glueck, Katie, *Politico,* November 8, 2013
(http://www.politico.com/story/2013/11/ken-cuccinelli-bright-spot-young-voters-99568.html)

[109] Blackburn, Scott, *PolicyMic,* November 7, 2013
(http://www.policymic.com/articles/72427/think-young-voters-are-liberal-election-2013-shows-you-could-be-wrong)

[110] Hohmann, Josh, *Politico,* May 10, 2013
(http://www.politico.com/story/2013/05/dem-strategist-warns-party-in-decline-91172.html)

[111] Hohmann, Josh, *Politico,* May 10, 2013
(http://www.politico.com/story/2013/05/dem-strategist-warns-party-in-decline-91172.html)

[112] Hohmann, Josh, *Politico,* May 10, 2013
(http://www.politico.com/story/2013/05/dem-strategist-warns-party-in-decline-91172.html)

[113] Huston, Warner Todd, *Breitbart,* March 19, 2014
(http://www.breitbart.com/Big-Government/2014/03/19/Millennials-Don-t-like-Gov-t-Any-More)

[114] Fournier, Ron, *the Atlantic,* August 26, 2013

(http://www.theatlantic.com/politics/archive/2013/08/the-outsiders-how-can-millennials-change-washington-if-they-hate-it/278920/)

[115] College Republican National Committee Report, 2013
(http://www.scribd.com/doc/145471237/Grand-Old-Party-for-a-Brand-New-Generation)

[116] College Republican National Committee Report, 2013
(http://www.scribd.com/doc/145471237/Grand-Old-Party-for-a-Brand-New-Generation)

[117] Wilson, Woodrow, reprinted by Hillsdale College in "Woodrow Wilson and the Rejection of the Founders' Principles," by Pestritto, Ronald J., 2012
(https://online.hillsdale.edu/document.doc?id=313)

[118] Gillespie, Nick, *The Daily Beast,* July 10, 2014
(http://www.thedailybeast.com/articles/2014/07/10/hey-boomers-millennials-hate-your-partisan-crap.html)

[119] Ekins, Emily, *Reason,* July 10, 2014
(http://reason.com/poll/2014/07/10/64-of-millennials-favor-a-free-market-ov)

[120] Trende, Sean, *RealClearPolitics,* July 2, 2013

[121] Trende, Sean, *RealClearPolitics,* July 2, 2013

[122] Trende, Sean, *Realclearpolitics,* July 2, 2013

[123] Enten, Harry, *The Guardian*, February 15, 2013
(http://www.theguardian.com/commentisfree/2013/feb/15/seniors-republican-young-people-democratic)

[124] Holt, Mytheos, *The Blaze*, December 5, 2012
(http://www.theblaze.com/stories/2012/12/05/with-young-voters-republicans-must-give-up-on-social-issues-or-give-up-altogether-poll-data-suggests/)

[125] Enten, Harry, *The Guardian*, February 15, 2013
(http://www.theguardian.com/commentisfree/2013/feb/15/seniors-republican-young-people-democratic)

[126] Miller, Zeke, *Time*, May 9, 2013
(http://swampland.time.com/2013/05/09/millennial-politics/)

[127] Enten, Harry J., *The Guardian*, February 26, 2013

[128] Miller, Zeke, *Time*, May 9, 2013
(http://swampland.time.com/2013/05/09/millennial-politics/)

[129] *The Pew Research Center*, February, 2010
(http://www.pewsocialtrends.org/files/2010/10/millennials-confident-connected-open-to-change.pdf)

[130] *The Pew Research Center*, February, 2010
(http://www.pewsocialtrends.org/files/2010/10/millennials-confident-connected-open-to-change.pdf)

[131] Hohmann, Josh, *Politico*, May 10, 2013
(http://www.politico.com/story/2013/05/dem-strategist-warns-party-in-decline-91172.html)

[132] Experian Simmons Fall 2011 NHCS Adult Survey 12-month, Accessed online via Navigation Partners, LLC on November 20, 2013
(http://www.navigationpartnersllc.com/hispanic-millennials-vs-hispanic-thirty-somethings-how-they%E2%80%99re-different/)

[133] *The Pew Research Center*, February, 2010
(http://www.pewsocialtrends.org/files/2010/10/millennials-confident-connected-open-to-change.pdf)

[134] Ekins, Emily, *Reason*, July 10, 2014
(http://reason.com/poll/2014/07/10/64-of-millennials-favor-a-free-market-ov)

[135] *The Pew Research Center*, February, 2010
(http://www.pewsocialtrends.org/files/2010/10/millennials-confident-connected-open-to-change.pdf)

[136] Fournier, Ron, *the Atlantic*, August 26, 2013
(http://www.theatlantic.com/politics/archive/2013/08/the-outsiders-how-can-millennials-change-washington-if-they-hate-it/278920/)

[137] Fournier, Ron, *the Atlantic*, August 26, 2013
(http://www.theatlantic.com/politics/archive/2013/08/the-outsiders-how-can-millennials-change-washington-if-they-hate-it/278920/)

[138] Payne, James L., *The Foundation for Economic Education*, April 21, 2011
(**http://www.fee.org/the_freeman/detail/can-government-manage-the-economy**)

[139] *MarketingCharts*, September 24, 2013
(**http://www.marketingcharts.com/wp/television/data-dive-us-tv-ad-spend-and-influence-22524/**)

[140] Ailes, Roger, *Speech to Bradley Foundation*, June 13, 2013
(**http://www.realclearpolitics.com/articles/2013/06/13/fox_new s_chairman_ailes_awarded_bradley_prize_118796.html**)

[141] Shafer, Jack, *Reuters*, August 15, 2013
(**http://blogs.reuters.com/jackshafer/2013/08/15/news-never-made-money-and-is-unlikely-to/**)

[142] McArdle, Megan, *Bloomberg*, August 20, 2013
(**http://www.bloomberg.com/news/2013-08-20/how-democrats-may-lose-their-media-edge.html**)

[143] McArdle, Megan, *Bloomberg*, August 20, 2013
(**http://www.bloomberg.com/news/2013-08-20/how-democrats-may-lose-their-media-edge.html**)

[144] DellaVigna, Stefano and Kaplan, Ethan, *The Fox News Effect: Media Bias and Voting*, The Quarterly Journal of Economics, August 2007.
(**http://emlab.berkeley.edu/~sdellavi/wp/FoxVoteQJEAug07.pdf**)

[145] Gerber, Alan S., Dean Karlan, and Daniela Bergan, "Does The Media Matter? A Field Experiment Measuring the Effect of Newspapers on Voting Behavior and Political Opinions," Yale University, 2006.

[146] McArdle, Megan, *Bloomberg*, August 20, 2013
(**http://www.bloomberg.com/news/2013-08-20/how-democrats-may-lose-their-media-edge.html**)

[147] McArdle, Megan, *Bloomberg*, August 20, 2013
(**http://www.bloomberg.com/news/2013-08-20/how-democrats-may-lose-their-media-edge.html**)

[148] Peterson, Paul E., Howell, William, West Martin, *The Wall Street Journal*, June 4, 2012
(**http://online.wsj.com/news/articles/SB1000142405270230364 0104577440390966357830**)

[149] Beckner, Gary, *The Wall Street Journal*, June 24, 2013
(http://www.forbes.com/sites/realspin/2013/06/24/americas-teachers-have-a-choice-and-this-includes-not-joining-a-teachers-union/)

[150] Shields, Mark on PBS *NewsHour*, Accessed Online on Nov. 15, 2013
(http://www.realclearpolitics.com/video/2013/11/16/david_brooks_im_really_struck_by_obamas_low_poll_numbers_and_the_anti-washington_sentiment.html)

[151] Hayward, John, *Human Events*, November 26, 2013, Accessed Dec. 12, 2013
(http://www.humanevents.com/2013/11/26/new-study-confirms-80-million-more-obamacare-insurance-cancellations-on-the-way/)

[152] Bradley, Donald and Canon, Scott, *Kansas City Star*, November 2, 2013
(http://www.kansascity.com/2013/11/02/4594291/young-people-the-key-to-obamacare.html)

[153] Powers, Kristen, *USA Today*, March 19, 2014
(http://www.usatoday.com/story/opinion/2014/03/18/millennials-democrats-republicans-liberal-independent-column/6577645/)

[154] Fournier, Ron, *the Atlantic*, August 26, 2013
(http://www.theatlantic.com/politics/archive/2013/08/the-outsiders-how-can-millennials-change-washington-if-they-hate-it/278920/)

[155] Fix the Debt, PR Newswire, October 25, 2013
(http://www.prnewswire.com/news-releases/poll-broad-support-for-comprehensive-plan-to-fix-the-national-debt-229284901.html)

[156] Fix the Debt, PR Newswire, October 25, 2013
(http://www.prnewswire.com/news-releases/poll-broad-support-for-comprehensive-plan-to-fix-the-national-debt-229284901.html)

[157] Aziz, John, *Yahoo News*, August 16, 2013
(http://news.yahoo.com/chinas-economy-wont-overtake-americas-anytime-soon-080500603.html)

[158] CIA World Fact Book, 2013

(https://www.cia.gov/library/publications/the-world-factbook/rankorder/2127rank.html)

159 Sizemore, Charles, *Forbes,* November 12, 2013
(http://www.forbes.com/sites/moneybuilder/2013/11/12/china s-demographic-collapse/)

160 Pei, Minxin, *Foreign Policy*, Jul/Aug 2009
(http://www.foreignpolicy.com/articles/2009/06/22/think_again _asias_rise?page=full)

161 Evans-Pritchard, Ambrose, *The Telegraph*, May 8, 2013
(http://www.telegraph.co.uk/finance/comment/10044456/China -may-not-overtake-America-this-century-after-all.html)

162 Evans-Pritchard, Ambrose, *The Telegraph*, May 8, 2013
(http://www.telegraph.co.uk/finance/comment/10044456/China -may-not-overtake-America-this-century-after-all.html)

163 Evans-Pritchard, Ambrose, *The Telegraph*, May 8, 2013
(http://www.telegraph.co.uk/finance/comment/10044456/China -may-not-overtake-America-this-century-after-all.html)

164 Foroohar, Rana, *Time,* April 10, 2014
(http://time.com/57158/chinas-growing-debt-problem/)

165 Snyder, Michael, *Right Side News,* January 21, 2014
(http://www.rightsidenews.com/2014012133773/us/economics/ the-23-trillion-credit-bubble-in-china-is-starting-to-collapse-global-financial-crisis-next.html)

166 Foroohar, Rana, *Time,* April 10, 2014
(http://time.com/57158/chinas-growing-debt-problem/)

167 Plumer, Brad *The Washington Post,* July 16, 2013
(http://www.washingtonpost.com/blogs/wonkblog/wp/2013/07 /16/a-simple-clear-explanation-of-chinas-economic-woes/)

168 Plumer, Brad *The Washington Post,* July 16, 2013
(http://www.washingtonpost.com/blogs/wonkblog/wp/2013/07 /16/a-simple-clear-explanation-of-chinas-economic-woes/)

169 Davis, Bob, *The Wall Street Journal*, September 29, 2013
(http://online.wsj.com/news/articles/SB1000142405270230479 5804579099640843773148)

[170] Davis, Bob, *The Wall Street Journal*, September 29, 2013
(http://online.wsj.com/news/articles/SB1000142405270230479
5804579099640843773148)

[171] Pei, Minxin, *Foreign Policy*, Jul/Aug 2009
(http://www.foreignpolicy.com/articles/2009/06/22/think_again
_asias_rise?page=full)

[172] de Jonquieres, Guy, *CNN*, October 24, 2013
(http://globalpublicsquare.blogs.cnn.com/2013/10/24/why-
china-isnt-an-innovation-powerhouse/)

[173] de Jonquieres, Guy, *CNN*, October 24, 2013
(http://globalpublicsquare.blogs.cnn.com/2013/10/24/why-
china-isnt-an-innovation-powerhouse/)

[174] Pei, Minxin, *Foreign Policy*, Jul/Aug 2009
(http://www.foreignpolicy.com/articles/2009/06/22/think_again
_asias_rise?page=full)

[175] Lenzner, Robert, *Forbes,* April 25, 2013
(http://www.forbes.com/sites/robertlenzner/2013/04/25/40-
largest-u-s-companies-founded-by-immigrants-or-their-children/)

[176] Pofeldt, Elaine, *Forbes*, June 26, 2013
(http://www.forbes.com/sites/elainepofeldt/2013/06/26/first-
generation-immigrants-dive-into-entrepreneurship/)

[177] Scott, Ian E., *Forbes,* September 6, 2013
(http://www.forbes.com/sites/realspin/2013/09/06/want-to-
create-american-jobs-remove-american-barriers-to-immigration/)

[178] Scott, Ian E., *Forbes,* September 6, 2013
(http://www.forbes.com/sites/realspin/2013/09/06/want-to-
create-american-jobs-remove-american-barriers-to-immigration/)

[179] BBC News, May 14, 2013
(http://www.bbc.co.uk/news/business-22524597)

[180] Serwer, Andy, *Fortune,* September 5, 2013
(http://money.cnn.com/2013/09/05/news/economy/energy-
boom.pr.fortune/index.html)

[181] LeBeau, Phillip, *CNBC*, April 18, 2013
(http://www.cnbc.com/id/100651692)

[182] Sirkin, Harold, *Business Week,* April 25, 2014
(**http://www.businessweek.com/articles/2014-04-25/china-vs-dot-the-u-dot-s-dot-its-just-as-cheap-to-make-goods-in-the-u-dot-s-dot-a**)

[183] Sirkin, Harold, *Business Week,* April 25, 2014
(**http://www.businessweek.com/articles/2014-04-25/china-vs-dot-the-u-dot-s-dot-its-just-as-cheap-to-make-goods-in-the-u-dot-s-dot-a**)

[184] Mizokami, Kyle, *War is Boring,* April 30, 2014
(**https://medium.com/war-is-boring/the-chinese-military-is-a-paper-dragon-8a12e8ef7edc**)

[185] Trende, Sean, *RealClearPolitics*, August 14, 2013
(**http://www.realclearpolitics.com/articles/2013/08/14/are_republicans_really_out_of_step_119590.html**)

CPSIA information can be obtained at www.ICGtesting.com
Printed in the USA
LVOW09*1534201114

414763LV00003B/4/P